My Father's House

Bethany Dawson

LIB
ERT
IES

NORTH

For Sam

You are neither here nor there,
A hurry through which known and strange things pass
As big soft buffetings come at the car sideways
And catch the heart off guard and blow it open.

— Seamus Heaney, 'Postscript'
from *The Spirit Level* (1996)

One

The temperature gauge in the car read 25 degrees. Traffic was at a standstill on the Drumcondra Road and wound like a long, shiny snake through the northern suburbs, to the Holy Child Church on the outskirts of town where the motorway started. It was Friday and the sun was shining at an awkward, afternoon angle that Robbie could not block with his sun visor. With one hand on the steering wheel, he used the other to shade his eyes so that he could negotiate the congestion. The pavement baked and students found shade under the cherry blossom trees while they waited for the bus. Robbie was suffocating from the warm, stagnant air in the car and the traffic's lethargic pace. Forcing himself to sit back, he rested his elbow on the open window and tried to relax.

Once he was on the motorway and had passed the airport, the traffic thinned. He tried to imagine he was following signs for Drogheda and the tightness in his chest subsided. He played through the scenario in his mind: he was going to interview one of the finalists for *Ireland's Got Talent* for the paper. She would be a gymnast, or an opera singer, or a young ventriloquist who spoke through a puppet ostrich. Her family would be gathered in the two up, two down council house and there would be plenty of plated custard creams to go round. It would be a one-hour job, including time to snap a few pictures of the girl and her puppet in front of the neighbour's hanging basket.

The turn off for Drogheda branched to the left and he distracted himself by fiddling with the iPod Hannah had bought him for Christmas. Whether his fingers were too big, or the buttons too small, he never ended up listening to the song he wanted. He thought wistfully of the days when his CDs were stored in a pocket on his visor, and there was no messing around with cigarette lighters and radio transmitters. With the device on shuffle, a Spanish guitar twanged from a set of albums designed to provide European background music for social get-togethers. Robbie cringed at the thought of dinner parties with Hannah's friends where she served Moules Marinière as a viola sounded from the hallway; or the time they had eaten gnocchi to the dulcet tones of an Italian opera. The guitar started to annoy him and he turned the whole thing off.

Friends had told him how much the road to the North had changed. It now bypassed Dundalk, where traffic had once crawled through the town centre, and skirted the feet of the Mourne Mountains in dual carriageway all the way to Belfast. He thought it would make it easier if it felt like an entirely different road, but the closer he got, the worse he felt. Even the weather seemed to conspire against him, with great, grey clouds gathering in the distance and the sun of the city fading in his rear view mirror.

The newspaper he worked for had recently hired a journalist from Northern Ireland, who had come into Robbie's office one afternoon to work out if they knew any of the same people. Robbie immediately disliked him. He talked about Belfast as if it were New York, calling shopping centres 'malls' and flats 'apartments'.

'The best part is,' he had said, oblivious to Robbie's attempts to ignore him, 'that all that religious, political stuff doesn't faze people as much any more.'

When he laughed, his top lip caught on his two front teeth, which jutted out from his gums. Robbie later regretted how he had stared the youth down and refused to share the joke.

By the time he reached the roundabout in Newry, the sky looked ready to burst. People were running across car parks; women gathered their dresses at their sides to stop the wind from getting beneath them and men looked knowingly at the clouds. Within several minutes, the rain fell so fast that even with his windscreen wipers on the highest setting, Robbie still found it difficult to see where he was going. Glad of the distraction, he sat forward and concentrated on the road ahead. Cars were moving so slowly that he calculated his journey from door to door would be just shy of four hours, as long as it would have taken before the new road was constructed.

As he passed the blue towers of Fane Valley, he marvelled at how very little seemed to have changed. Aside from a few new developments, the houses were as squat and unsubstantial as he remembered, some with small gardens and many with none at all. A sign for *Banbridge Portadown Tandragee* was mounted at the roadside of a new junction and he squinted through the rain as he passed a car garage. A small man in overalls hunched under the corrugated iron roof of his shed talking to a young couple.

The rain was starting to ease when he turned off the dual carriageway. The old ruin stood in the corner of the field and he could picture his younger self poised with plastic sword in the archway. It looked as misplaced as it always did, with the Stevenson's double-storey mansion on one side and the busy A1 on the other, but Robbie could remember well that once you were inside the crumbling walls, the noise of traffic and the view of houses disappeared. In that damp, secluded space he had become an explorer, a knight, a king or a hermit, and everything else became much less real or important.

With the car purring on the verge, he stepped out to get a closer look. The rain had stopped and for a brief second the clouds parted and watery sunlight escaped, exposing the gaps in the walls, as well as the graffiti that had not been there when Robbie was a boy. With his ankles wet from the grass, he leant on the gate that led into the field. He was taking deep breaths, enjoying the country air laced with the faint staleness of the nearby chicken farm, when half of a rainbow took form in front of him. It was difficult to make it out, and if he had not been staring at that exact spot he might never have noticed it, but it was unmistakably arched from the grass beside the ruin towards the road. The violet edge was faint and the colours ran into one another and smudged across the sky.

Back in the car, Robbie adjusted the rear view mirror to face him. Never quite satisfied that he was a good-looking man, he had allowed his hair to grow out so he might at least be mistaken for an interesting one. He pulled at his fringe until his cow's lick had been tamed and it curled neatly behind his ear, then ruffled the back of his hair, which was soft and wavy from being washed that morning. One last scan of his face confirmed that he was clean-shaven and the puffiness had gone down from around his eyes. He turned his attention to the shirt he had deliberated over that morning, buttoning and unbuttoning it at the top before making sure it was tucked neatly into his jeans and not too strained around his stomach. His grandmother had often remarked that carrying a bit of weight was a sign of good health and he hoped that his mother would not take as negative a view of his expanding waistline as Hannah did.

He kept his eyes straight ahead as he passed the farmhouse, swerving to avoid a long branch of the cypress hedge that had broken free like an unruly lock of hair. At the crossroads he was forced to glance briefly towards the western edge of the farm where the front gates blew in the wind and the overgrown verge made it difficult to negotiate the junction safely. In his absence, a new bungalow had been built on the opposite corner to the farm. It was whitewashed and plain, with a tarmac driveway that bent steeply to the road and a young crab apple tree starting to blossom over the entrance. A tractor was approaching from the right and Robbie watched it go through the junction and continue past the farmhouse, the driver bouncing around, a flat cap tight on his head. With one last glance to his left, he caught sight of the sign, rusted around the edges and almost completely obscured by ivy: Larkscroft Farm.

Two

Robbie had stumbled upon a career in journalism and found, surprisingly, that he was quite good at it. He was inquisitive and had a dogged determination, but words did not come easily to him. Every time he sat down to write an article, he suffered the kind of self-doubt that left him staring at the cursor on his screen for minutes on end. The story would come to him at first like a large ball of wool, the kind that his grandmother used to knit into jumpers that scratched the skin. He would spend several minutes examining it for a way in, a loose thread, an angle that would unravel the tale into something controversial to shock his readers. However, the ball was often impenetrable and nothing remained but for him to move on to something else.

Although Robbie's column commanded an impressive following compared to some of the other feature writers, he approached it without any real belief, but intent on repaying some sort of debt that hung over his head. His debt was tangible, predictable: a mortgage, two cars and a luxury week in the Seychelles when Hannah fell pregnant and his hopes of travelling the world were dashed. He had not chosen the title of his column, 'The Culture Vulture'. In fact, he strongly disliked it and on many occasions had petitioned his boss for a change. The image of himself as a large bird with pink jowls waiting hungrily to sort through the carnage of a theatrical disaster, a pop sensation gone bad or a second novel that fell far short of the first bothered him. It was not the cynicism that he was opposed to, nor the mocking tone that he was allowed to take which he never otherwise got away with; it was the idea of picking through the remains of something that was already dead. It was morbid and dark, but his boss viewed all the letters of complaint as evidence of success and so refused to change the name.

As he again checked the directions to his mother's new house, the picture of a big, black scavenger flapped around in his mind. The house was tucked away behind the main street in Donaghcloney and the huge sycamore trees lining the entrance gave it a grand appearance. Robbie marvelled at the space afforded to each property on the road. He had become so accustomed to the apartment blocks springing up like weeds all over Dublin, that the roomy gardens and driveways were a novelty. His mother's home had a large back garden sloping down to a river. It was situated in such a way that none of the windows in the house next door looked into it, and plants of all shapes and sizes created a hedge around the outskirts of the front garden. Robbie stretched when he stepped out of the car and smelt something damp and spicy coming from the flowerbed. Bright pink butterbur flowers sprouted from between their huge green leaves, nodding politely at him in the breeze. He recognised the fragrance from where they grew wild on the riverbank near the farmhouse.

'Robbie?'

He had his head in the boot, digging out his laptop bag and suitcase. It was a male voice, deep and purposeful. Robbie stood back to observe a stocky man in his early fifties, with cropped, brown hair, smiling at him.

'Welcome,' he said, extending his hand. 'I've heard a lot about you.'

Robbie looked over the man's shoulder to make sure he was at the right house, before dropping his shoulder bag and taking his hand.

'My name is Adam,' he said. 'Please come in. Maggie will be home soon.' Adam lifted the laptop bag and left Robbie standing in the driveway with a creased forehead. Maggie? He let out a deep breath, closed his car boot and followed the man into the house.

Adam moved around the kitchen with familiarity, lifting the plates of the Aga to set the kettle on to boil, laying out china cups and pouring milk from a carton into a jug. Robbie stood with his hands on his hips, not sure where to put himself in the room. If it hadn't been for the Aga and the baskets of dried flowers in the cabinets, he could have been in anyone's kitchen. Evidence of his mother was minimal; instead, the trinkets of a much more interesting and vibrant woman littered every surface: mismatched pieces of pottery on the dresser, huge black and white feathers displayed in a vase, jars of pickled vegetables standing beside a row of herbal teas and in the corner a monk's chair looking rather pleased with itself, with cushions plumped up and ready to sit on. It was not at all what he had expected and unlike the farm in every way. It was grand where the farm was humble, colourful where the farm was sage and cream throughout, dusty where the farm was astringently clean and, strangest of all, welcoming where the farm seemed impatient for people to leave. With everything so unfamiliar, it almost made sense that a man in black jeans and a cardigan several sizes too large was pouring tea into china cups. It was all comfortably out of place and when Robbie heard his mother's steps in the hallway, he had no idea what kind of woman he was about to encounter.

'Here you are,' Margaret said, pushing her fringe back with her sunglasses. 'Ah, and I see Adam has sorted you out for tea. Wonderful. Just let me throw these bags down somewhere and I'll come and join you.'

When she left the kitchen, Adam held a biscuit tin out to Robbie and arched his eyebrows. Robbie held his stare, his eyes narrowing on the tuft on Adam's chin that seemed so at odds with his neat hair and cardigan. Their eyes remained locked as Robbie reached for a Rich Tea and returned Adam's smile sarcastically. The man seemed not to notice as he pulled out a chair at the table for Robbie. His calloused hands on the biscuit tin suggested that his work was manual.

'My son,' Margaret said from the doorway. Adam pressed himself against the fridge to allow her to pass. Swallowing his biscuit, Robbie stood up to embrace her. There was nothing familiar in her scent, only the faint smell of talcum powder and the residue of a wet raincoat.

'Would you look at the cut of you,' she said, holding him at arm's length.

'I can't say the same for you, Mum. You look incredible.'

Time had changed them both, and each needed a moment to take it in. Did she see the flecks of grey in his hair, the extra weight around his waist and the tiredness that had seeped into his skin from the strain of a new baby? Was his scent the same, or had he picked up other smells in their five years apart? She was studying him as though his face held the answer to a question only she knew. Her eyes were hungry and had committed to being blue after years of watery indecision. Although her hair had been grey since he could remember, she had cut and styled it, making her seem younger than ever. The elastic-waisted skirts that had once been her wardrobe staple had been replaced with jeans, and everything else about her was bright and colourful, from her eyeshadow to the pink scarf that she had tossed over one shoulder.

Satisfied that they had found one another beneath all the years of aging, they hugged again and Margaret moved off to find a more suitable plate for the biscuits.

Three

Standing at the top of the bridle path, Robbie could see the Mourne Mountains in the distance, cloud settling around their middle to resemble the sherbet spaceships of his childhood. It was early morning and the curtains had been drawn on most of the windows he had run past. After years of sore knees from running on concrete through the busy Dublin streets, to run in the country again gave Robbie the energy to make it the full eight miles to the path without stopping. The air was easier to breathe, despite it being so cold that it caught in his throat and made his lips dry. At the edge of a new season, the countryside seemed glad to leave the winter behind. Although the roads were quiet, Robbie noticed houses where once there had been fields and huge signs erected by developers to warn of the residential buildings to come. There were more cars in driveways and, as he passed Sam Johnson's house, he could just make out the blades of a helicopter through the trees. Despite words like economic downturn and credit crunch being in full circulation, not everyone seemed to be suffering.

The hedges along the bridleway were glossy from the rain, the beginning of spring regrowth giving them an untidy appearance. Bullocks charged the fence to see what he was doing and the sound of a rooster carried across the field from the farmhouse. As he walked around the corner, Robbie could see the front field of the farm with the two cherry blossom trees splayed against the pebble-dashed wall of the house. The grass was being kept at bay by two fat sheep who, at that moment, were rubbing their bodies against the steel legs of a property developer's poster board. *Brand New Development* the sign read in large print.

Despite his mother saying that the farm had fallen to pieces, Robbie struggled from his vantage point to notice anything different. Perhaps the pink of the cherry blossom had distracted him from the bare earth in the flowerbeds and the empty pots at the front door. Or maybe on closer inspection there would be cracks in the walls, cobwebs in the doorframes and mould flourishing in the small, damp bathroom. Blackthorn bushes were flowering ahead of schedule along the boundary fence between the house and the field, and the white petals, from a distance, looked like snow. He could see that the hawthorn tree had not been trimmed for a long time and almost obscured the big, green gate into the front field where the sheep were.

Memories of trying to trim the thorny branches with hedge cutters came back to him. It was impossible not to emerge scratched and bloody from the deceptively beautiful tree that drooped with red berries in the autumn and boasted bright, white flowers as early as February. The tree had been planted by his great-great-grandmother to disguise what was then the outside toilet, before his grandfather tacked a proper lavatory on to the hallway. Over the years the trunk thickened and cracked, like a scab with a pink wound beneath it that had almost healed. The branches started to stray towards the gate where they interfered with its opening, and Robbie's instructions had been to cut it to within a foot of the gate's hinge. For a boy of nine, that was a difficult task.

He rubbed his hands, pulled his hat down to keep more of his forehead warm and started jogging down the hill.

∞

Showered and sitting on the bed to put his socks on, Robbie

looked out the window of his mother's spare room to the back garden where wind chimes hung from the trees and a pond was taking shape beside the decking. His mind wandered to the jars of pickled vegetables on the kitchen dresser. It seemed such a strange thing for his mother to eat, considering her cooking had been so plain when he was a boy. Images of thick slices of bright pink gammon came to mind with a pineapple ring on top that his father had picked up with the end of his fork as if it were a dead fish. Robbie had hated gammon but he and his sisters had cleaned their plates, making particular mention of the pineapple. Most nights it was chewy pieces of beef or lamb, the cheap cuts that refused to soften in spite of being ferociously boiled for hours. His mother always managed to cook the cabbage until it wilted pathetically on their plates, and the carrots until they were soggy and dissolved in their mouths.

Later, when his father did not join them for dinner, they were lucky to get a dry piece of toast and a slice of cheese with the mouldy edges cut off. Sometimes his sister Wendy would drag a stool into the pantry and hand Robbie a tin of tuna and a packet of crisps which he would make into mini sandwiches for their younger sister, Elizabeth. It was not until Robbie left home that he ate things like lasagne, chicken pie, curry and beef burgers. His first year away from the farmhouse was marked in his memory by the food he ate and the discovery that dinner need not be something to 'get through' as if it were a school exam or a dental appointment. With that in mind, the pieces of pickled cucumber, carrot, onion and pepper were not things he could easily imagine his mother enjoying. He stopped himself. His brain was still wired to find an angle and the pickled vegetables were a stray end he was trying to use. With his shoes laced and his hair combed, he looked long and hard at himself in the mirror and determined not to start unravelling the story.

The kitchen was warm from the Aga and smelt of maple bacon and coffee. Something about being in his mother's house made him feel less sure of himself. He was glad Hannah and Amy had stayed at home. Hannah had not been happy that he was leaving, especially because he did not know how long he would be away. It was difficult to watch her wrestling with her desire to cling on to him and the knowledge that if ever he had a good excuse to leave, it was then. Coming from a family so tight that they almost strangled one another, Hannah had found it hard to accept that Robbie had no contact with his. At first she had prodded and pushed for information; her questions were delicate and unassuming. Soon, though, she grew frustrated, and her suspicion and his impatience met in an argument that left him feeling guilty and her with no option but to let it go.

After pouring the strong, black coffee into one of the mugs laid out on the table, Robbie sat down and rolled his shoulders in their sockets to get rid of the tension in his back. He was quite relieved not to play husband, father, brother and son all at the same time; concentrating on the last two would be hard enough work he was sure.

'Sleep well?' his mother's voice sounded behind him. 'You're pulling at your neck like the bed did some damage last night.'

'Not at all. I slept fine, thanks.'

'Good. Bacon?'

She pulled a tray out of the top oven where thin strips of bacon had curled around charred tomatoes and mushrooms covered in herbs. While she served Robbie some food, the front door banged and Adam could be heard in the hallway on his mobile phone.

'You'd think he smelt it,' Margaret said, her lips turned down in mock disapproval. 'Eggs?'

'Yes, please.'

'I hope you like those tomatoes; I tried a new recipe using balsamic vinegar.'

'They look great.'

Robbie buttered the toast that she had set on his plate and

tried to plan the day ahead. He had half-expected his sisters to arrive the night before, eager to see their estranged brother. They were conspicuous by their absence and it made Robbie uneasy.

'I suppose I should see the girls,' he said, shovelling his scrambled eggs into his mouth.

'Yes, son, I suppose you should,' she said.

At that moment Adam padded into the room in his socks. Robbie greeted him but quickly turned away when he placed a hand on the small of his mother's back. The night before Adam had barbequed sausages out on the decking while Robbie sat with his mother in the kitchen. Her command of the stove had been impressive as she sprinkled a pinch of something over a tray of chunky vegetables set to roast in the oven and bent over pots to taste their contents with a teaspoon before smacking her lips with glee. Her face was flushed and Robbie could see a deep contentment in it that was unfamiliar.

Margaret's way of evading questions and filling the silence with endless babble left him with the feeling that they had talked a lot but said very little. Around the dinner table she told endless tales about people from the town he did not know, stopping occasionally to allow Adam to chip in. Later she dragged out an old photograph album and set it squarely in Adam's lap, patting the sofa beside her for Robbie to sit down. It was strangely comforting to see the photos but bizarre to hear his mother's running commentary that was so at odds with his own memory.

'This was the day wee Robbie found an injured pigeon in the garden and brought it to the back door like a cat. Poor creature had its wings broken and despite our best efforts, it died. Ah, the girls were heartbroken. Lizzie's a sensitive thing and we had to have a funeral and everything,' Margaret said, stroking the part of the picture where Elizabeth's wet cheek was turned to the camera.

The photo was of Wendy aged twelve sitting on the dry stone wall that ran around the perimeter of the back garden. Her head was bent over her cupped hands where the pigeon lay with feathers slicked down by Elizabeth stroking its breast. Robbie was in the background, standing behind his sisters, elevated on his tiptoes to look at the bird.

He had been kicking about in the orchard, jumping on the apples that had fallen too soon from the trees. A strong smell of garlic came from the wild ramsons growing by the hedge and the day had been warm enough to be outside without a jumper. With little else to amuse him, he turned his attention to next door's prize-winning racing pigeons, who favoured his family's orchard as a resting place. After collecting a handful of stones, he took shots at them as they flew in from the field to feast on the seed balls his mother had made. He had not expected to hit one; when his father went shooting, he would often return empty-handed and go on about how smart the birds were. But, sure as hell, on his fourth attempt he heard a dull thud and watched the feathers lingering in the breeze after the bird had fallen to the ground. His mother smacked him so hard on the backs of his knees that it was difficult to bend them for a week. She marched him next door to admit to the murder and stood back as their neighbour shouted for what felt like hours.

Adam had moved on to the next page of photographs, examining one of the two girls kicking water at each other in the stream. Robbie tried to catch his mother's eye but she had averted her gaze and muttered 'He was a good lad' so softly that he almost missed it.

Four

The phone call had come two weeks earlier. Elizabeth's voice had been watery, immediately conjuring memories of his childhood: the smell of the farmyard after the pigs had marched through it into the truck bound for the abattoir; digging in the undergrowth for conkers, their prickly exterior just how he imagined a landmine would look; and hanging over the farm gates sucking ice pops in the summer. With cheeks full of freckles and hair that refused to be tamed, Elizabeth was as close to a brother as Robbie could have hoped. Her knees were always grass-stained, at the age of eight she could stalk a fox, and her long skinny legs took her to the tops of trees in record time.

'Wendy said you'd to make up your own mind whether to come back or not,' she said. 'But really, Robbie, I'm going to ask you anyway. Things seem to be falling apart and it hasn't mattered until now that we don't work so well as a family. It's not right that you aren't here.'

Hannah had been popping her head through the living room door intermittently and eventually wedged it open with a phone book so that she could eavesdrop better. He was cross about that. He had started to resent this lack of privacy, which had gradually seeped into their married life, along with urinating with the door open and wearing her mouth guard to bed. Did she like it when he scooped the dirt from beneath his toenails with the tip of a biro lid? What about his threadbare underpants or the days he skipped brushing his teeth? Two years in and he could not remember when those issues had been decided or how he and his wife had become so uncomfortably comfortable with one another.

Even as he told Elizabeth that he would think about it, his decision to go had been made. Whether his six-month-old daughter screaming in the background, or the raised eyebrows of his wife had anything to do with it he could not say, but the relief in his sister's voice when he phoned her back the next day convinced him that he had done the right thing.

ℭ

It was not until midday, when the sun was directly overhead and wisps of cloud lolled about the sky that Robbie had summoned the courage to visit his father. When he paused again at the crossroads, Robbie watched the tall stems of cat's-tail that stood like toothbrushes in the grass at the roadside. He imagined his mother arranging them in one of her stemmed glass vases, reminding the girls never to buy flowers when so many beautiful ones grew wild. Robbie indicated right and pulled up to the farmhouse. The paint had peeled on the gate to show the bright green that his mother had hated so much, and the gate scraped along the ground when Robbie opened it. Once sandy in the summer and muddy when it rained, the driveway had been tarmacked when he was eleven. He remembered how old he was because it was his first year at the Academy and he had to catch the bus into Banbridge from the bottom of the road. His father used to shout at his mother for turning the steering wheel of her car when it was stationary; he said it tore up his good tarmac. Now the driveway was pockmarked, and water had collected in the ruts from the rain that had fallen overnight. The petals from the cherry blossom hid the worst of it, carpeting one whole side of the driveway where Robbie parked.

As he waited at the front door, Robbie could hear the rooster crowing out the back and the sheep had come to the fence at the sound of his car. Several minutes passed and his father did not appear, so he made his way through the small shed that led to the yard. The boiler roared to life and the oil fumes caught in the back of his throat. It was a warm, little, in-between room with a cobbled floor and lots of pegs in the stone walls on which to hang things. Old fishing nets that reeked of the sea were piled in the corner and a collection of rusty garden tools leant against the wall like weary old men taking a break. The back door of the house was locked and the curtains drawn to prevent him looking in. After scuffing his feet on the green lichen-like growth that covered the yard, he made his way to the barn with four small hens and a proud rooster at his heels.

He was forced to a halt when he saw that the three large greenhouses were overrun with weeds, and the wind had blown panes of glass onto the concrete. The irrigation lines were barely visible and ivy had wound its way up the trunk and branches of the peach trees. On closer inspection he could see where the herb garden had germinated to take over an entire corner of the first and largest greenhouse. Mint was the most dominant of the herbs and its smell hung in the air when Robbie rubbed the leaves between his fingers. Parsley and coriander had gone to seed, the latter tall and flowering between the broken glass. As he dug deeper, he found several tomato plants that had bent under the weight of their fruit and were all but buried beneath bright yellow dandelions and grass. All the signs of defeat prepared Robbie for the version of the man whom he found stooped on a stool beneath the huge body of a cow. He was in one of the pig sheds with a small table lamp powered by an electric cable from the house. His back was turned and Robbie watched him for a moment, slow as he tugged at the teats to send short bursts of milk into the silver pail while the smoke rose from his pipe. The green tweed coat he wore was too big for him now and his body looked shrunken and small inside it.

'Hello, Father.'

John paused without turning around. The cow exhaled. After wiping his hands on his trouser legs, John pushed the stool back and used the cow to steady himself.

'I wondered if you'd come,' he said, finally turning to face his son.

They observed one another.

'I thought I should,' Robbie said, looking away.

His father shrugged and moved towards the door. Robbie stepped aside and then followed him as he shuffled back to the house.

'Staying a while?' his father called over his shoulder.

'A few days.'

'I mean now. Will you have some tea?'

'Yes, please.'

The kitchen was clean but a faint smell of sour milk lingered. It was cold inside and the linoleum on the floor was coming apart in places so that the old stone showed through.

'You sit down,' Robbie said, moving towards the kettle.

'I will not indeed,' his father said. 'I can make a cup of tea just fine.'

He pulled a cord so that the blinds were lifted and more light could come in. Despite it being a good day outside, the kitchen did not get the sun until late afternoon when it shone orange and red through the side windows of the house.

'You've kept the place well,' Robbie said.

'Yes, well, Wendy is always about, washing this, ironing that. If it weren't for her . . .'

Robbie could see how Wendy had tried to keep the house as it was. In a chipped vase on the windowsill, switches of gorse blossomed yellow and, when the blind was lifted, he could see that there were no streaks on the glass. The furniture was the same, only stained more and glued together in places. Everything felt smaller and so separate from Robbie that he could hardly remember living there. He had not carried the details well in his mind and was glad of it.

The kettle shook in his father's hand as he poured water into the teapot and Robbie fought not to feel sorry for him. With mugs of tea in front of them, they sat face to face at the kitchen table. Robbie had not noticed the yellow tinge to his father's skin until then, spreading from the neck of his jumper upwards like a suntan. His eyebrows closed in on each other like two thick caterpillars and there was hardened sleep in the corners of his eyes. The psoriasis on his neck seemed to have worsened but Robbie could not be sure if that was owing to the absence of a shirt collar that had once hidden it better. He reminded Robbie of the old men in Dublin who walked to the post office once a week to get their living allowance. Layered with jumpers and dragging their feet in ill-fitting shoes, the men would make guttural noises to one another while rolling their own cigarettes or scratching their heads. Perhaps it was the few days' old stubble on his cheeks or the torn edges of his clothing which made him appear similar, but Robbie found it difficult to believe that this was his father.

'How are you feeling?' Robbie asked. His father had not offered him any milk for his tea and he did not want to ask. Instead, he blew on the surface of it until he could take a sip.

'Fine, considering.'

'What's the prognosis?'

'It's in my pancreas. You don't last long if it's in your pancreas.'

Robbie nodded.

'Can they operate?'

'Depends. I'll have one of those scans on Wednesday – a CT I think you call it. They do that to see if it has spread. Doctor says it can get into your lungs. If it has, there's nothing they can do.'

'And if it hasn't?'

'They can operate, I suppose. There's a name for the operation, funny-sounding. Can't remember though – memory's not what it used to be.'

He bent his head to his cup and sucked the tea through his teeth.

'Are you in pain?'

'Not from the cancer. Knees are stiff these days. Just old age taking hold of me. But nothing much to complain of besides that.'

The silence between them made Robbie uncomfortable and he started talking about Hannah and Amy, taking care to skirt around issues like the wedding his father had not been to or the baby pictures he had never got around to sending.

'Amy?' he said. 'After my mother?'

'Yes.'

His father's eyes were wet and he started to speak but then stopped.

'I'd better get on,' Robbie said.

'Aye, right you are.'

John did not stand up as Robbie poured the rest of his tea down the sink and backed out of the kitchen. With the front door closed behind him, Robbie breathed in the spring air and heard one of the sheep bleating.

Five

Elizabeth and Wendy were at their mother's when Robbie got back. He heard Wendy's twins shouting in the hallway; they had taken their socks off to slide along the polished parquet floors from the bathroom to the kitchen and did not pay any attention when Robbie came through the front door. Wendy summoned them to meet their uncle. He had several nieces and nephews on Hannah's side and now a daughter of his own, but Robbie was distinctly uncomfortable around children. The pressure to say something relevant or pitched towards their particular age-group was too much for him and he often endured silence in response to his questions. Wendy was only newly married when he left for Dublin and the two fully formed children wrapping themselves around her legs were evidence of the years that had passed between then and now. As his sister tried to coerce the two boys to speak and expressed both embarrassment and frustration when they didn't, they peered at Robbie and he tried to calculate their age. In his mind, children between the age of three and six were difficult to categorise, so after a few basic calculations he pronounced them four years old.

'Four and one month,' said Simon, stepping out from behind his mother so that Robbie could see the direct resemblance to Wendy's husband.

'You're not my uncle,' the other one said.

'Excuse me?' said Robbie, raising his eyebrows towards his sister.

'Mum said we had one aunty, no uncles. She said—'

'Okay, that's enough, boys, go back to your games while we have some more tea,' said Wendy, shooing them out the door.

Elizabeth and his mother were sitting around the kitchen table, nursing half-drunk cups of tea and exchanging looks. Wendy stood with hands on her hips.

'We've been waiting for you,' she said. 'The boys are clean mad from hanging about as you can see.'

'Sorry, I didn't know you were coming. I wouldn't have gone out, if I'd known.'

Her hair was cut short and the weight from childbirth was clinging to her middle, refusing to be hidden by a blouse. When he reached his arm around her shoulders, Robbie felt her flinch. She patted his back before taking a seat at the table.

'Lizzie, come here and give me a hug.'

His younger sister smiled and stood to embrace him. She was just as he remembered: long hair held loosely at the nape of her neck by something that looked as if it would be better used to hold paper together, and clothes that were both fashionable and unassuming.

'So good to see you,' her voice came muffled by his coat.

'He arrived yesterday,' Margaret said. 'I was out with the Maguires and when I got in I thought someone had parked in our spot by accident. We don't know anyone with so fancy a car. Then I saw the plates and knew it was Rob, didn't I, son?'

Robbie nodded and Margaret started to give the details of Mrs. Maguire's problems with the housing executive. Her voice was high-pitched and strained. Once or twice during her monologue, he caught Elizabeth watching him, her face softer than their older sibling, but equally unreadable.

'We were discussing the race before you came,' Elizabeth interjected when Margaret paused for breath. 'Wendy's Paul is mad keen to take the boys but you know what that place is like – all burger vans and country folk who drink too much.'

Robbie laughed and shook the teapot in his mother's direction.

'Don't be a snob, Liz. I just don't want them interested in motorbikes, that's all,' said Wendy.

'You have to let them be children. Little boys like that sort of thing,' Margaret said.

Wendy sat upright. 'This isn't a mothering issue; it's a safety issue. Someone dies every year at that bloody race.'

'All the more reason for you to go along and supervise.'

'I might go this year,' Robbie said. 'I could look out for them.'

He watched his older sister purse her lips.

'That won't be necessary. Anyway, you've never been interested in motorbikes.'

'I know. It's for work.'

'Work?' Margaret asked, pouring tea into the mug she had set in front of him.

Robbie realised that none of the three women knew what he did.

He cleared his throat.

'I write a newspaper column. It's got a culture and arts focus normally but I'm doing a special series while I'm up here.'

'Really?' his sisters echoed.

'Yes, with the new roads opening things up a bit between the North and South, people are taking more of an interest in what's going on across the border. The only way I could get time to come up was to agree to write about the "lesser-known Northern Ireland", as my editor calls it. The motorbike race is just part of it.'

'Sounds great,' Elizabeth said.

'Well, keep an eye out for any young men taking the corners too tight and ending up dead in a field,' Wendy said, scowling.

Elizabeth opened the biscuit tin on the table and passed it to Robbie. He met her eye and smiled.

'I've got to get going,' Wendy said, holding her hand over her mug as Elizabeth tried to top up her tea. 'Will you be back for long?' she asked Robbie, busying herself with a large, black coat.

'I'm not sure, I suppose it depends . . .'

'Well, I'll maybe see you again.'

Robbie laughed. 'Of course,' he said, but she had already opened the door on her children and started ordering them out of the house. Margaret followed her and the twins to the front door.

'Don't worry about her,' Elizabeth said. She lowered her voice. 'How'd it go with Dad?'

'All right, I suppose. He's not looking great, is he?'

'It's been a while since I saw him. Did you talk much?'

'Not much. The house is a bit run down. It was really strange being back there again.'

Elizabeth nodded. 'We can't get much out of him about the cancer.'

'He didn't tell me any more than you did on the phone. I suppose there isn't much more to say about it.'

'I've been meaning to read up on it,' she said, hanging her head. 'I just can't get round to it.'

'That's ok. What about Wendy?'

'What about her? She won't say a word about it. She just busies herself with things that need doing around the house and pretends that it isn't really happening. Mum won't allow his name to be spoken in the house, so it's all a bit ridiculous if you ask me.'

Robbie nodded.

'Did you see the sign?' she asked.

'Yes.'

'Nobody knows anything about that either. We didn't even know he had sold until Wendy drove past one day and saw the billboard in the front field. That was five months ago and still nothing.'

'How much did he get for the place?'

'We don't know. I've asked around but people are just guessing. Some say over a million, others say less.'

'It's hard to believe that it's gone, just like that.'

'I know. Wendy was so angry; I think she saw herself living there. Mum almost crashed the car when she saw the sign. I have to tell you about it. I was in the car with her coming back from the butcher's. She hardly ever drives up that way but the other road had been closed for roadworks. Anyway, it was the day the guys from Johnson's put it up and the neighbours were watching from their gardens. Mum was in such a tizzy that she pushed the accelerator instead of the brake when she came up to the crossroads, and Heather Bishop from number nine was knocked clean off her bicycle.'

Elizabeth put her hand over her mouth to hide a laugh and checked to see where her mother was.

'If Heather hadn't been wailing so loud that even Dad came out to see what the fuss was about, it would have all been quite funny. Of course Mum didn't stick around but I called later that night to make sure poor Heather was all right.'

'It's very odd though, isn't it?' Robbie said. 'I remember back when we were little, a fella from a big firm in Belfast came sniffing round the land and Dad chased him off the doorstep, saying that he would only sell over his dead body.'

'Well . . . '

They heard their mother's step in the hallway and a car pulled into the driveway.

'That must be Adam,' Margaret said as she came through the door. 'I need to go upstairs to freshen up. Tell him I'll be down in a minute.'

The front door opened and Robbie managed to catch his sister's eye long enough to communicate his confusion over the man's presence.

'Good afternoon,' Adam said, warming his hands against the Aga.

'Having a good day?' Elizabeth asked him.

'Yes, yes. I'm just here to collect Maggie.'

'She'll be down in a minute.'

He looked towards the stairs and then sat down opposite Robbie.

'I'm helping a friend with his van at the race today. He's been complaining that the engine is making a noise.'

'The race isn't until Saturday,' Elizabeth said.

'I know. Some of the guys set up early and Irwin likes to get a good spot.'

'You're an engineer?' Robbie asked.

'Adam is a jack of all trades,' Elizabeth said.

'I'm good with my hands,' Adam said, lifting them up and laughing. 'My father was a mechanic and my uncles were all very successful tradesmen. I pick things up quite fast and make my way as a handyman. I'm actually working on Maggie's Mini in my spare time.' He pointed out the window.

'Really?' said Robbie. 'But it's been broken for well over ten years. It's ancient.'

'Well you'll have to have a look at it sometime.'

'Maybe.'

Six

Robbie had not seen the sun shine in Lurgan since the day Martin O'Keegan was shot. It had been a cold, bright day in late September 2005. The trees were starting to turn and some of the greengrocers had pumpkins carved for Halloween hanging from their tarpaulins. Martin had asked him to drive down from Belfast for the weekend. Robbie had protested at first – there were people he had arranged to meet that weekend – but Martin insisted that what he had to tell him was better than any leads Robbie might be following.

The park had been full when he arrived, crowded with families throwing stale bread to the swans and solitary men with their unleashed but obedient dogs. Robbie waited for his colleague on a bench set back from the lake. The weeks leading up to that weekend had been particularly busy after compromising photographs of a well-known Orangeman had turned up on his desk. Robbie had been working late into the night to craft something that would make the headlines that weekend, and he would not have agreed to meet anyone had Martin not insisted.

As lead political journalists, Martin and Robbie often worked together on big stories, although most of the time Martin covered County Armagh and the lower half of County Down, while Robbie was based in Belfast and expected to travel to Antrim several times a month. Martin had been with the paper for years and reluctantly took Robbie on as a trainee.

Martin's uneasiness that afternoon was contagious and the usual care he took when rolling his cigarettes was abandoned as he squinted into his tobacco pouch and produced ungainly roll-ups. He complained about the sun, so they moved indoors. Robbie tried to lighten the mood by reminding his colleague of their first visit to a pub. It had been a bar Robbie had never heard of before and when he remarked on this, Martin told him it was mixed and then stared at him for a long time.

'I'll explain one thing from the word go,' Martin had said, leaning in towards Robbie. 'My wife's a Protestant and I'm a Catholic. All this sectarianism in our society is what drives me as a reporter. If you want to get anywhere in this job, son, you'd better not pick a side – that's all I'm saying.'

Robbie's sombre expression at this, teamed with an upper lip wet from his Guinness, made Martin laugh.

'You've a lot to learn,' Martin said. 'You'll come and meet the wife this weekend and we'll talk some more.' With that, he had thrown some money on the table, lit his cigarette and left the pub.

Martin laughed at the memory of their younger selves but his joviality was unconvincing and made Robbie nervous.

Five years on, Lurgan had a cosmopolitan feel to it, with several European restaurants on the High Street and a bridal boutique in the centre, where tiara-clad mannequins competed for space in a window display. Whether it was the sun, or the effect of time passing, the Shankill Parish Church seemed less menacing in its position at the top of the town and Robbie found a parking space alongside it. The solicitor's office was a short walk and Robbie had little time to plan what he would say before he was ushered into the office.

'Robbie Hanright, well I never!'

'How are you doing, Colin?'

The men shook hands enthusiastically before sitting down.

'It's been an awful long time. Eight years – maybe more?'

'I've lost count myself. How's the family?'

'Grand, everyone's well. I'm sure yours is happy to see you.'

'Yes, it's good to catch up with everyone.'

'Pity about the circumstances, I'm awful sorry.'

'Thanks, Colin. That's actually why I'm here.'

'I thought as much. What can I do for you?'

'I'm sure you know about the farmhouse being sold?'

Colin nodded.

'Well, we were all a bit shocked to tell you the truth and no one really knows what's going on; how much did it sell for? where's all the money gone? you know, that sort of thing. Our father is hopeless at communication, as you are well aware, and I suppose, well, I thought that maybe—'

'I could tell you?'

'Well, yes actually.'

Colin sighed, picked up a biro from his desk and started clicking the end of it.

'As a solicitor, I am bound to protect the privacy of my clients, you know that, Robbie. I understand how difficult that is when I'm also a family friend and know more than I probably should but there's nothing I can tell you, I'm afraid.'

'What are we supposed to do?'

'Well, there are two options. You can either persevere with your father and try to discuss the matter with him, or you can wait until his passing, God rest his soul, and accept his wishes.'

When Robbie met Colin's eye, he recognised the pity that had been so familiar to him when he was a child. It was not the first time he had considered the fact that his father was going to die but it was the first time he had reacted to it. Not with sorrow, tears or fear, but with frustration and a sense of embarrassment. He felt sixteen again and wanted nothing more than to laugh in Colin's face and run out of the room. Instead, he smiled politely and assured the solicitor that he understood and was grateful for his time. He tried not to tarry in the handshake that Colin used to convey his sympathy and took a convenient fit of coughing in order to leave the reception in haste.

ॐ

When Robbie got back to the house, Adam's van was in the driveway. He followed the sound of music to the bottom of the back garden where Adam had established a small business fixing cars. Robbie found him elbow deep in the engine of his mother's old car, with Van Morrison blasting out of a battery-powered radio attached to the wing mirror. Adam's head bobbed enthusiastically and he lifted his spanner to beat the time in mid-air.

'That's a classic 1989 Mini Flame,' Robbie shouted over the music.

Adam jumped and fiddled with the switches to lower the volume.

'Sorry, Robbie. I didn't know you were there.'

He blushed and wiped his hands on his overalls.

'Great song,' Robbie said.

'Yes.'

The men avoided eye contact.

'I'm not far off finishing this one,' Adam said, turning towards the open belly of the Mini.

'Am I right that this is a Mini Flame?'

'Yes, that's right,' Adam said.

'It's ancient.'

'So Maggie keeps telling me. I haven't been beaten by a car yet and I'll get it on the road if it kills me.' He winked.

'It hasn't been driven for over ten years, Adam.'

'Pity that.' Adam was staring into the engine. Robbie didn't know much about cars, but as he walked around the outside of the Mini, he saw that the rain had rusted some of the paintwork around the door hinges and the back left tyre was missing, with three bricks in its place.

Adam closed the bonnet, moved to the driver's door and

lowered himself into the car.

'Get inside,' he said to Robbie.

Robbie folded his body into the small seat and Adam leant across him to open the cubbyhole on the dusty, walnut dash. He produced a silver hip flask, unscrewed the top, wiped the mouthpiece with his sleeve and passed it to Robbie.

'What is it?' Robbie asked.

'Sloe Gin. I made it myself last year and it's just about ready for drinking.'

The windows in the car were rolled down so they could lean their elbows on them. The sound of bees in the tree above their head was audible over the music.

'I understand you being suspicious of me,' Adam said.

Robbie looked out over the garden. A magnolia tree offered white flowers like open hands to the sky and pigeons were perching on the fence.

'It must be very strange to come back and find everything so different.'

'It's not so bad.'

Adam lit a cigarette and exhaled out the car window.

'My job makes me a bit suspicious,' Robbie said, trying to explain.

'You work for a newspaper. Isn't that right?'

Robbie nodded. 'It's hard to turn my brain off sometimes.'

'Well I hope you find a way to turn it off. For your mother's sake,' he said, pointing the cigarette at him for emphasis.

Robbie waved the smoke away, muttered in agreement and left the car.

Seven

In the summer, when the temperature rose and the countryside hedges grew until they needed taming, Robbie's father would drag the lawnmower from the shed, oil it and spend an entire day cutting the grass in the front field. Two strands of an electric fence kept the sheep in one half of the field while the other half was designated as a garden. The neighbours would look on as he pushed the heavy piece of machinery around the acre of land until the sun was setting and a hefty mound of cut grass had accumulated on the compost heap. Robbie remembered smelling it from the road on his way home from school; the sharp earthy scent that ushered in barefoot games of rounders. As the most sensitive sibling, Elizabeth cried at the beheading of all the meadow flowers and the fewer places to hide. Wendy would take her by the shoulders to tell her that most of them were weeds and were better off dead.

'It's your father,' Margaret said, handing Robbie the phone at the breakfast table.

'Dad?' he said into the receiver.

'Would you be about to do a job or two? No matter if you're busy, I just remembered you were up and I have a thing or two needs doing—'

'I'm free today. What do you need?'

'The lawn is getting good and long; it'll need a strimmer if I don't get it cut soon and it's a good day for it today. I've some animal business to attend to, so won't have the time to work at it myself . . .'

'Of course, what have you got now for cutting it?'

Robbie saw his mother rolling her eyes.

'Sure you know what I've got – the same one I've always had. No good buying a new one when the aul one is working fine. If you're not bothered—'

'No, that's fine. I'm sure it'll be grand. I'll finish off my breakfast and head over.'

'Youse still at your morning meal?'

'Yes, late start today. Just getting some eggs and bacon—'

'Right, right. Sure I'll see you when I see you,' he said and put down the phone.

Robbie looked at the receiver and laughed. His mother, who had been hovering beside him throughout the conversation, turned away to load the dishwasher.

'Wants me to cut the front field,' he said.

'It's good of you to help him,' Margaret said over her shoulder. 'It'll take the best part of the day, mind you.'

'I suppose it's the least I can do.'

Margaret slammed the dishwasher shut.

'Don't you do that, son. Don't you come over all guilty. If you cut the grass, cut it for the right reason.'

'And what are the right reason? Surely guilt isn't so bad at this stage.'

He watched his mother running a dishcloth through her hands.

'Sit down,' Robbie said softly.

'Families are funny things,' she said, sitting beside him. 'All this time I've wanted him to suffer but getting what you want doesn't ever feel the way you hoped.'

Robbie wiped his palms on his trouser legs.

'I'm just cutting his grass . . .'

She looked at him and smiled.

'I know. It's the first year he hasn't been fit to do it himself.'

They looked at each other and her eyes were soft. Robbie cleared his throat and stood up.

'I'd better hit the road.'

'I'll see you later,' Margaret said, licking her finger and lifting crumbs from the table.

ꝏ

When Robbie arrived at the house, the lawnmower was sitting in the middle of the driveway and his father's car was gone. The sun was dappled on the grass beneath the cherry trees and daffodil stalks were beginning to rot in the flowerbeds. If it had been Robbie's garden, he would have waited at least another fortnight before cutting the field. There were only a few inches of re-growth and it was a long way off needing a strimmer but when he looked across the road he saw that all the neighbours had done theirs. He manhandled the large piece of machinery down the steps into the field and checked the engine for petrol. Finding it full, he started the back-breaking task of pulling the chain to get the motor started. It coughed and spluttered for the first few pulls before roaring into life and jerking forwards. Robbie started in the top right-hand corner of the field that slanted steeply down to a hedge at the bottom.

The task of putting his weight behind the heavy lawnmower to urge it back up the incline demanded all his physical strength but gave licence to his mind to wander. He looked at the house in its pebble-dashed glory and tried to remember a time when he was happy inside its walls. On a sunny day it was easier to recall mornings when the kitchen was bright and the lace curtains billowed like ship sails from the open windows, or summer evenings when the sun would set outside the living room window and make the whole room orange; but it was impossible to see himself in his memories. Where was he standing when the sun was setting? Was it against the window, watching the sky change colour from blue to pink to deep, dark red? Or had he been engrossed in a book or newspaper until his mother caught his attention and he registered the light in the room? In the mornings, did he notice the lace curtains and the fresh country air, or was he so full of longing to leave that it was lost on him until twenty years later when he was digging for the reassurance of happier times?

It had not been a conscious decision to cling to the better memories of his childhood. It had just happened when Hannah came along and the possibility of a brighter future dragged his scowling face away from the details of his past. Now, standing in the middle of the poorly part-mowed field, in front of the house that was hiding all the reasons he had run away, he wondered if it would be possible to hold the past and present in tension.

'You must have started late,' his father shouted from the back entrance to the field.

'Don't jump up on me like that.'

'Drove into the yard. I thought you'd see me pass by on the road.'

'No.'

Robbie continued to push the lawnmower while his father walked the cut section of the field, inspecting his son's work.

'You need to be lining up better,' he shouted over the machine. Robbie pretended not to hear him. His father scuffed his feet a few times before walking slowly towards the house.

After two hours of mowing, the sun was directly overhead and Robbie turned the lawnmower off to go in search of some food. Even in the height of summer, his mother would cook a big pot of stew for his father coming in from the field. No matter how many hours the pot had bubbled on the stove, the meat would still refuse to break down in Robbie's mouth and the carrots tasted too much like the earth they had been dug from. He took the plastic bag that his mother had slipped to him on his way out of the house. It contained half a loaf of bread, some cooked ham and a punnet of cherry tomatoes.

'I suppose you're wanting fed?' his father said when Robbie met him in the backyard. He was on his knees surrounded by pieces of wood and wire mesh that he was using to construct a chicken coop.

'What do you need that for?' Robbie asked.

'Foxes got two of my birds last night. The coop needs reinforcing if I don't want to lose the whole lot.' He squinted in the sunlight. 'What's that there?'

'Some food for sandwiches. Will I make us up something?'

'I needn't have bothered going out to the shops,' he said, throwing the piece of wood in his hands onto the tarmac. 'You tell your mother I can feed myself just fine and anyone else who comes my way.'

'It's just a bit of bread, Dad, no big deal,' Robbie said, reaching his arm out to help his father stand.

'I don't need your help,' he snapped, waving the arm away. 'You eat your sandwiches. I'll get stuck in to a chicken and ham pie.'

'Well if you're having pie—'

'No, no, I'm sure sandwiches will do you just fine.'

Robbie walked towards the house while his father rinsed his hands beneath the outdoor tap. Once in the kitchen, he let out the breath he had been holding and set about buttering slices of bread.

Robbie sat opposite his father at the kitchen table, watching as he took the packaging off his store-bought pie.

'Do you want it heated?' Robbie asked.

'I do not.'

Robbie had finished his sandwiches by the time his father had cut into the slimy contents of his lunch. With few teeth left to speak of, John pressed his gums against the food and rolled it around his mouth before swallowing.

'I'm glad I don't need to mow around that there sign,' Robbie said, motioning to the front field. 'I don't know why they had to erect such a huge eyesore in the middle of your field.'

'It's not my field any more.'

'Even still.'

'Sure they're not the least bit concerned about an old codger like me renting the house he sweated to build. They're already planning fancy flats and all sorts.'

'You must have got quite a packet for it,' Robbie said quietly, concentrating on picking a tomato from the punnet.

'It's not worth much to them now. Johnsons own most of the land from here to Enniskillen and they say that the bottom is about to fall out of the market.'

John was smiling as he chewed.

'Anyway, you may just let the grass grow up round that sign, son. Not much else you can do.'

 

The sash windows of the farmhouse had been painted shut for the winter months, leaving the air upstairs stale. Robbie could hear his father banging at something in the yard while he pushed open the door of his old bedroom and watched as clouds of dust were disturbed from the furniture. All was as he had left it five years before and he wondered had anyone even set foot in the room since then. Piles of notebooks covered his desk, their edges withered from the heat of the small box room. While running his fingers over old newspapers, he found holes in the pages where his articles had been. A dried pritstick was upended beside his scrapbook that he once imagined showing off to future employers in London or New York. He flipped forward to the last entry, only to see Martin staring back at him, his eyes bright and face relaxed, with an inset photo of his grieving widow. He slammed the book shut, put it back on the desk and covered it with the newspapers.

His bedroom window overlooked the front field and the cluster of houses at the crossroads. The cherry blossoms were being stripped from their branches by the wind and Robbie could see dark clouds approaching from the north.

'Fearless and relentless' was the briefing they were given. 'Those words must become your mantra,' his boss had told the rest of the staff from behind his big, oak-panelled desk. Then again at the funeral: 'Martin was fearless and relentless in his exposure of criminal activity in Northern Ireland.' And everyone had nodded and cried a bit, looking up at the picture projected on a screen above the priest's head. All Robbie could think was that Martin would have hated having his picture displayed like that. The photograph was splashed across newspapers, shown on television and used by policemen on their door-to-door search for more information. In the majority of newspapers the story fizzled out in a matter of weeks, but Robbie's former colleagues were unrelenting in their coverage and for the first few months in Dublin, Robbie followed the stories on the internet, learning the sordid details about the men responsible for the murder who had never been arrested.

'Robbie?' his father shouted from the kitchen. He grabbed his scrapbook from the desk, shut the door behind him and took the stairs two at a time.

'What were you doing up there?'

'Just nipped in to get this,' he said, holding the book up for his father to see. 'I need to keep a record of all my work.' He wiped his forehead.

John narrowed his eyes and flicked his fingers towards the field.

'Grass won't cut itself, son, and there's rain on its way, so ye' may get out there sharpish.'

It was four o'clock when the first drops of rain fell. Robbie had managed to cut three-quarters of the field and was trying to negotiate the trunk of the cherry tree when he had to haul the lawnmower to shelter. In the living room he found his father asleep in an armchair, his arms folded across his chest and a blanket on his lap.

There was something disarming in his pose that made Robbie stand still and watch him. He had never considered how elderly his father was now, choosing in his absence to remember him as a younger man with darker, fuller hair and a defined jaw line, a man who walked purposefully around the farmyard and had enough brute strength to destroy solid wooden chairs during his drunken rages. In the majority of Robbie's memories, his father had his back turned. He was either leaving the house for the pub, or retreating into an outside shed with a bottle of something. Yet in front of him sat a withered version of a man, riddled with disease and shrinking in clothes that at one time had fitted him so well.

Outside the window behind his father, Robbie caught sight of the silver birch tree planted when his parents first moved into the house. Its trunk, which once peeled like cracked paint, had developed deep fissures with age and made it seem as though a darker, more malevolent tree was being exposed beneath the silvery bark. It was in a line of even older birch trees that had been planted by the generations of Hanrights before him. They were drenched and the new leaves bent under the force of the downpour. The dark, damp afternoon started to depress Robbie and had his father not woken at that exact moment and scowled across the room at him, he might have started to light a fire or to find something to prevent the cold air from seeping in beneath the doors.

'I've done as much of the grass as I can. The lawnmower is in the shed,' Robbie said, clearing his throat.

John tossed the blanket off his lap as if it were a cat making a nuisance of itself and made as if to stand up. The effort of it seemed too great and he looked as though he were in pain.

'Are you all right?'

'Yes, fine. That will be all.'

'What about a cup of—'

'No.'

Robbie remained standing. He was not sure what he was waiting for: a petition for help, a thank you for the work he had done that day, or just a basic acknowledgement that he was there after so many afternoons when he was not.

'Very well,' Robbie said, turning to leave. 'See you later.'

'Don't forget . . .' Robbie heard his father shout after him. He came back into the room.

'What?'

'Your book.'

'Right.'

Eight

On his arrival at the Tandragee 100, Robbie found Adam at his friend's sausage van, a half-caravan, half-motorvan vehicle with a large extendable flap on one side which opened so the two men could hand out hotdogs. The men were standing with arms crossed in the van's cramped interior.

'No one seems to be beating down the door for your sausages,' Robbie said when Adam introduced him to Irwin, a man wearing a shirt spattered with oil who, from the colour of his skin, looked as though he holidayed abroad.

'Just you wait until they have a bit of drink in them,' Irwin said.

'Good to see you, Robbie,' Adam said. 'Would you like a hotdog?'

'Go on then.'

'I believe you're up from Dublin,' Irwin said, hacking at a bread roll.

'That's right.'

'I've never been.'

'Never?'

'Nope.'

'It's a great city," Adam said, nudging his friend. 'You should try it.'

'I've heard it's not too bad, but I'd never convince the wife.'

'Maggie and I went to a great play in the Abbey. What was it called . . .'

'You were in Dublin?' Robbie quizzed.

'Ketchup or mustard?' Irwin asked, wiggling the bottles over Robbie's hotdog. Adam pretended he had not heard the question.

'Adam?'

'Yes? Sorry, what did you say?'

'You and mum came to Dublin and didn't call?'

'Come on, Robbie,' Adam said, motioning to Irwin to put ketchup on the hotdog. 'It was a couple of years ago. Maggie didn't think it was a good idea.'

'I see.'

Robbie took the hotdog.

'Thanks for this. I'll be seeing you.'

'Robbie . . .'

Without a backward glance, Robbie headed across the field into the gathering crowds.

It was not until he was among his own people that he recognised how much of an outsider he was in Dublin. Seeing old faces, eavesdropping on conversations about places he knew, and listening to his own dialect made him smile. Martin had described something similar from his time in Carlow.

'In many ways they are more like me,' he said. 'But they're not part of the community I was raised in. They didn't watch me ride my first bicycle or know the family well enough to tell me Ma that I'd mitched off school. Nothing beats coming home.'

He stood awhile at the fence, watching the racers bend their knees on the corners until they were almost in line with the road. The noise was deafening as brightly coloured bikers sped along the country lanes, accelerating on the straight sections and taking off on some of the smaller hills, much to the delight of their young fans. Hay bales were stacked along the roadside and some of the local farmers had erected bleachers in their fields for friends and family. It was impossible not to be infected by the adrenaline-charged atmosphere and Robbie was soon absorbed into a group of young men who worked in Hunter's Supermarket and had taken the day off.

By late afternoon the race was over and Robbie was squeezed into a picnic bench between a construction worker from Hamiltonsbawn and a trainee beauty therapist whose nails were so long that they curled the entire way around her beer bottle. He had misplaced his notebook and pen somewhere between the finish line and the field and the bottom of his jeans had absorbed so much water from tripping into puddles that the skin on the inside of his knees was raw. Bottles of cider kept appearing in front of him from the plastic bags on the grass and his stories about life in Dublin made the whole crowd laugh until one young man started to vomit in the hedge and the hilarity of it occupied them for longer than it should have.

When the sun had set and the youths dispersed, Robbie extracted himself from the hairdresser who had fallen asleep on his lap and started the thirteen-mile walk home. Somewhere between Gilford and the bridge over the River Bann, his legs gave up and the grass at the roadside seemed as good a place as any to have a rest. As he lowered himself to the ground, Robbie's footing gave way and he fell heavily on his side. He felt a sharp pain in his right arm and winced, struggling to manoeuvre himself so he could lie on his other side. His phone was in his jacket pocket but it took him almost ten minutes to extricate it with his left hand and press the redial button before his head rolled back onto his rucksack.

Watery images of his daughter disappeared in his dreams before Robbie could get a good look at her face. As he dipped in and out of sleep, she would be waiting for him, sometimes sleeping peacefully, sometimes shivering without her blankets and beyond his reach. Where was Hannah? Didn't she hear their daughter crying? The sound of a car engine terrified him as he tried to get to the Moses basket in which his daughter lay completely still. He could not see if she was breathing and her tiny arms were out of his reach. Someone was calling his name and his head fell backwards as the collar of his jacket was wrenched from above.

'For God's sake, Robbie, would you wake up before your mother has a heart attack.'

When he opened his eyes he saw Adam. The smell of his breath reminded Robbie of his father as a young man and he wondered whether his mother still bought the same toothpaste. He could hear his mother somewhere in the background.

'Are you hurt?' Adam asked.

'No.'

'He's fine, Maggie,' Adam shouted over his shoulder.

'Fine? Then why is he lying beside the main road in the middle of the night?'

Adam lifted Robbie's arm and squatted beneath it, steadying himself on the footpath before lifting him to his feet.

'I don't need your help,' Robbie said, stumbling towards the hedge and grabbing a blackberry branch to steady himself. He winced as the thorns punctured his hand and the ache from his fall caused him to hold his right arm. Adam stepped closer to him.

'If you don't need my help, why did you phone?' He ran a hand through his hair. 'Listen. Forget about me. Forget about your pride. Just take my arm and sober up. Your mother and I have been out looking for you for the last hour and she could do without this sort of carry on. Do you understand?'

Robbie squinted towards the car. His mother had turned her head and all he could see was the collar of her coat and her elbow on the window frame. From the way her body was positioned, Robbie knew she was stroking her mouth with the back of her fingertips as if her words needed time to soften. As a young boy bundled into the back seat of a car on a Friday night, this was a stance with which he was familiar. It was how she sat outside the pub, waiting for her husband to emerge bleary-eyed and unrepentant.

Robbie cleared his throat, took Adam's arm and allowed him to open the back door of the car. The drive home passed in silence but Robbie managed to speak to Adam at the front door after his mother had gone upstairs.

'It's my arm,' he said.

'Yes,' Adam said. 'I will help you change your shirt first.'

ȣ

The clock on the dashboard read four o'clock in the morning. The lights on the Westlink lit the empty road, framed by the shadowy peaks of the Black Mountains.

It was the time of the night that Robbie had often seen as a young journalist when writing articles did not come naturally and he had to extract each word at a painstakingly slow pace. Cigarette breaks on the front step of his house often relaxed him enough to finish a sentence or come up with the adjective that had refused to be pinned down in the computer room. During those breaks he met a version of himself more honest and human than his waking self would have had him believe. He would admit to wrongs, confess his love, miss his mother and worry about the future. With each inhalation, the truth would be made clearer and resolutions would be formed, or habits broken that by eight o'clock in the morning would be forgotten on the walk to work.

While Belfast slept, he was confronted by a straight-talking version of himself who demanded that he pull himself together and stop allowing things like the smell of cut grass and the petulance of his older sister to have such an effect on him. The exit for the hospital came and he glanced at Adam.

'Thank you,' Robbie said.

Adam sighed.

'I care about your mother very much,' he said, after a long pause.

'I can see that.'

Robbie saw a triage nurse and was told that his wrist was broken. After an x-ray to confirm the break and a two-hour wait to see a doctor, his arm was plastered below the elbow and he was able to leave the hospital. The sun was up and remnants of conversation from the night before were coming back to him in the wrong order. He was ashamed to think of Adam holding a clean shirt open for him while averting his eyes in embarrassment and was glad Adam had not waited at the hospital with him. In the bus station, Robbie stood in front of the board looking between the Dublin and Dromore timetables. Two and a half hours and he would be in the city. He bought a cup of coffee and took out his phone.

'Hi love.'

'Robbie? You're up early.'

'Am I?' The clock above him read half past eight. 'Yes, I suppose I am.'

'Is everything ok?'

'Of course. I'm just . . . Is that Amy I can hear?'

'She's been up all night. I'm exhausted. Was there something else? Only I need to get her bottle made up.'

'No, no. You go on. I can talk to you later.'

'Right then.'

'Give her a kiss from me.'

Hannah gave a short, sarcastic laugh. 'Sure.'

'Bye now.'

Robbie lowered the phone and stared at it for several seconds. Checking for change in his pocket, he bought a ticket and went in search of the bus.

Nine

Margaret was waiting for Robbie in the square, tight-lipped and wearing a housecoat over her pyjamas. They drove in silence until they had cleared the town.

'Thanks for picking me up,' Robbie said.

'Where is your car?'

Her driving was fast and frightening.

'Tandragee.'

'How on earth did that happen?' she said, nodding at his cast.

He lowered his head. 'I don't remember.'

'Oh Robbie,' she said, sighing.

He drew patterns on the condensation-covered window. He was a schoolboy again, picked up by his mother in the square where the Ulster Bus left him after rugby practice. He would be slumped in the seat, grass-stained and shivering from all the dried sweat and, depending on the kind of day his mother had had, she would either start drawing him out of his teenage stupor, or say nothing and drive straight-backed and silent all the way home.

'Adam is a good man,' he said.

'Yes.'

As they passed the end of John's road, Robbie checked his watch.

'I'm supposed to take Dad to the hospital today.'

'How are you going to manage that?'

Robbie pressed his temple. 'I'll phone one of the girls.'

'Well, I can tell you Wendy is away with the boys on a school trip to the aquarium and Elizabeth is working until six o'clock.'

'Adam?'

Margaret laughed. 'Adam? Adam take your father to the hospital? Don't be absurd.'

'Well what do you suggest?'

'I don't know, son. It's got nothing to do with me.'

Robbie thought of his father preparing for the day ahead. He imagined him stiff-jointed and slow, buttoning up his shirt before eating his breakfast alone at the kitchen table. The farmhouse was never warm; even when the oil-fired central heating was installed, the windows leaked and the heat was sucked under the doors with a high-pitched whistle on windy nights. It was difficult for Robbie to imagine his father moving between the empty rooms of a house that had been a family home for generations. He had remembered his father as a larger man, both in stature and influence. Somehow the image of him shuffling, scowling and alone made it hard not to pity him.

'I can't let him down like this,' Robbie muttered.

'You should have thought of that last night.'

Margaret's tone was so unfamiliar that Robbie looked at her and expected to see someone else. They had pulled into the driveway and she stopped the car with such fury that it skidded on the gravel and sent clouds of dust into the air. Robbie waited in the passenger seat for several seconds after his mother had got out, trying not to be baffled by how forthright she had become. He looked from the empty driver's seat to the open front door of the house and back again several times, going over her words and replaying them in the fierce tone in which they were uttered. He had never heard his mother speak like that. As a wife she had been long-suffering; as a mother she was reserved. There used to be a vacancy in her gaze when something outside the window would captivate her for long periods of time. Her eyes would gloss over and when one of the children summoned her into their conversation, it was with a pained face that she turned to them and answered.

He followed her into the house. Managing the heavy front door with his left hand was difficult and he could see how frustrating the next few weeks would be. He was rummaging in the bathroom cabinet in search of painkillers when his mother appeared behind him.

'I will take you,' she said.

Robbie turned to face her.

'You don't have to, Mum.'

'Do you have another idea?'

'I haven't quite got round to it yet.'

'Here,' she said, opening a small drawer in the cabinet and producing a bottle of paracetemol. 'I'll be downstairs when you're ready.'

&

The flowerbeds in the front driveway of the farmhouse were cracked and dry, with several spindly rose bushes showing few signs of new growth. John stood with the hosepipe beside them. He was wearing an old navy suit and had made an effort to brush his hair over to the side to disguise his baldness. Robbie had chosen not to tell him that Margaret was driving them to Belfast.

There was a moment of recognition when they pulled into the driveway. Ex-husband and wife regarded one another through the car window, long enough for Robbie's father to soak his trousers and curse loudly. He was muttering under his breath and shaking the water from his leg as he lowered himself into the back seat of the car.

'Margaret,' he greeted her.

'John.'

Robbie swivelled to face him.

'Are you comfortable, Dad?' he asked.

'Perfectly.'

'Mum?'

'Stop fussing.'

Robbie caught his father's eye in the mirror.

'Your appointment is at eleven, right?' Robbie said.

'That's right.'

'In the oncology ward?'

'Yes.'

His father had closed his eyes and his mother rolled hers. Memories of car journeys to Donegal came back to him: the three siblings in the back seat, arms and legs strewn everywhere and an empty space between his parents. An image of his mother's hand resting on his father's thigh flitted briefly in his mind, so briefly that he thought he must have imagined it or willed it during one of his more sensitive moments. The destination was always the same – the Carrigart Hotel in Sheephaven Bay. His parents knew the owners, so that when the children were eating separately in the neon-lit kids' restaurant, his father had someone to talk to besides Margaret.

'Why did we go to Carrigart Hotel every year on holiday?' Robbie asked.

The question seemed to surprise his passengers. John started fumbling for the button to open his window and Margaret tightened her grip on the steering wheel.

'Your father liked the decor,' she said, casting a provocative glance over her shoulder.

John did not respond. His eyes were shut and his mouth opened and closed like a goldfish to take in gusts of air. To Robbie he seemed old and tired, a shadowy likeness of the man he remembered. The tables had so completely turned. No longer were the family creeping around in the presence of a tyrant, trying to find the elusive line, which once stepped over was impossible to recross; there was no fight in his father, nor was there any sense of victory for Robbie.

He turned on the radio and fiddled with the dial until he heard the unmistakable voice of George Jones on Radio Ulster.

Ten

'Will I draw you a diagram?' the gastroenterology consultant asked Robbie and John.

Robbie nodded without checking with his father. Whether he understood or not, Robbie was determined to know the ins and outs of the procedure, for his sisters' benefit if nothing else.

'I'll have to explain it to the girls, Dad,' he said while the consultant reached for a piece of paper and pen. His father scratched his neck with the impatience of a man who had better things to do with his hands. Robbie guessed that the doctor was Egyptian, although his accent was decidedly Northern Irish. His temperament was professional, though highly strung. His eyes were set deeply into his dark skin and thick black hair sprouted from his shirt-sleeves to cover his hands. After a few strokes of his pen, he had produced a diagram of the inside of a human body: the oesophagus, stomach, intestines, pancreas, liver and gall bladder, with several tubes connecting the liver to the duodenum. A thick black scribble around the pancreas was labelled *Tumour*; it was a childlike picture of the aggressive growth choking his father's bile duct and it made the whole thing seem farcical.

'As you can see,' he began, 'the tumour has wrapped itself around this little duct that transports all the bile from your liver into the intestines to be excreted. When that happens, the chemicals are released through your skin, causing jaundice, itching and all the vitamin deficiencies I told you about the last time. It also means that you aren't absorbing any fat, which explains the weight loss and pale faeces.'

John's face screwed up at the mention of bodily waste. The consultant then lifted a red pen to draw the journey that the camera would take down his throat, all the way to the blocked duct.

'We will then put a wire in here and insert a stent to widen this duct and allow the bile to get through,' the consultant said, dropping his pen on the table and sitting back in his chair. 'Does that all make sense?'

Robbie looked at his father, whose eyes had glazed over. 'Yes, thank you, doctor,' he said, folding the piece of paper. 'Can I take this?'

'Of course.'

'My sisters will want a re-enactment and my artistic skills aren't as good as yours.'

The consultant smiled and turned to John.

'Any more questions, Mr Hanright?'

'How many days will I have to stay here?' he asked, his voice clogged by phlegm. He cleared his throat and repeated the question.

'It depends on how well you respond; we need to observe you for at least twenty-four hours to make sure your liver function is okay and that you don't develop any further complications, but we'll do our best to get you out as quickly as possible.'

John was on his feet before the consultant could finish his sentence.

'Very well then,' he said over his shoulder on the way to the door, 'I'll be seeing you next week.'

'Thank you,' Robbie said as the door closed.

'Will you be accompanying your father?'

A large poster behind the consultant's head warned of the dangers of not following a stringent hand-washing policy. A young nurse was covered in green-coloured bacteria that she was spreading to the patients around her. Robbie thought of the tumour and all the space it was occupying inside his father and imagined his fear at having to stay overnight in a hospital for the first time in his life.

'We'll see' was all he said to the consultant before shaking his hand and leaving the room.

℃

'Where the hell is Margaret anyway?' John said as he shuffled down the corridor.

'You're going the wrong way, Dad,' Robbie said gently, taking his elbow to steer him back in the other direction.

'Don't you do that,' his father said, stopping Robbie.

'What?'

'Go all soft just because we're in here and you sat in on one of my consultations. Not that I even asked you to now that I mention it.'

'I thought you wanted—'

'I never said anything about it. Anyway, I'm just saying not to fuss about me or go all . . . all . . . Where is Margaret?'

He took off up the corridor, following the exit signs and muttering. Margaret had gone in search of the coffee shop. Robbie had told her to meet him at the entrance in twenty minutes and, as he caught up with his father and they made their way towards the sliding doors, Robbie could see Adam standing next to her. His father slowed his pace momentarily and Robbie thought he heard him curse under his breath, before he ploughed on, almost knocking into Adam on his way through the door.

'What are you doing?' Robbie said to his mother, holding her back by the arm.

'He finished early and needs a lift home.'

'You can't be serious.'

Robbie felt the colour flushing to his cheeks.

'It's my car and my choice. Perhaps our other passenger is the one with the least right to travel with us,' she said, voice lowered while Adam scuffed his shoes beside them.

'That *passenger* is your husband,' Robbie said.

'*Was*, Robbie, and I'd thank you to remember that.'

Robbie was left standing alone as Margaret linked arms with Adam and marched him in the direction of the car park. What had previously been background noise rushed in on him: teenage mothers hollering for a cigarette, geriatric patients wheeling their drip stands on the linoleum floors, coffee machines whirring and the subdued whispers of the ill and their family working out the details of their sickness in the same complicated ways.

&

'It was hideous. And she insisted on sitting in the front, of course, so poor Dad was left shoulder to shoulder with Adam in the back seat,' Robbie said, clinking his glass with Elizabeth's.

'It would be funny if it wasn't all so sad,' she said, leaning in towards the fire. 'Was there much chat?'

'Are you kidding? I nearly died from the exertion of trying to get a bit of non-confrontational conversation going, but you know Dad: he would argue over the price of soap.'

'Dear dear,' she said, lifting her glass to examine its contents. 'They all had to meet some time I suppose.'

'Well, I'd rather it hadn't happened in a confined space at seventy miles an hour. Something wrong with your drink?'

'Not strong enough,' she said, smiling.

'This place hasn't changed a bit,' he said, looking around at the whitewashed interior walls of the pub. A fire loaded with turf smoked in the grate and men drank pints around the small tables made of old Singer sewing machine desks.

'What is she playing at?' he said.

'Mum? I've given up trying to work that one out.'

'Can you blame her though, really?'

'I try my hardest not to,' Elizabeth said, draining her glass and standing to order another round. Robbie watched her at the bar, small beside the high-heeled beauties who had arrived too late to get a seat. He sensed that Elizabeth had been surviving too long on the edge of something messy and that his presence, and a few more rounds of gin, would give her licence to fall apart.

'Friday nights don't come cheap any more, I tell you,' she said, pocketing her loose change. 'What?' she said when he didn't respond.

'Nothing, it's just been so long since we've talked.'

She avoided his gaze.

'Tell me what the consultant said.'

Patting his jeans for the diagram, he laid it out on the table in front of her. She regarded it suspiciously.

'This is quite a simple diagram,' he assured her.

Elizabeth no more than nodded while Robbie regurgitated the doctor's explanation of the operation.

'Very good,' she said at the end, 'if it's going to make a difference.'

'He won't be in so much pain.'

'I didn't know he was.'

'Really?'

'I don't see that much of him, that's all. Wendy doesn't really talk about it either, and you know Mum,' she said, laughing.

'When did you see him last?' Robbie asked gently.

'Oh, I don't know really.' She looked about her at the pub filling up.

'Roughly speaking.' He pressed her.

She jutted her chin into the air and took a gulp of her gin and tonic.

'Christmas maybe,' she said. 'Although it could have been

earlier in December. Can't remember exactly.'

'Oh, Lizzie,' he said, unable to hide his surprise. 'I didn't know you were so out of touch. . .'

'Well there's a lot of things you don't know, Robbie. Perhaps you'd be better off not sticking around to find them out. What do you intend to do with all the knowledge anyway?' she asked, folding the diagram carefully.

She had lined up her next drink.

'Nothing. I don't have any intentions or expectations; you phoned me and I came, it's as simple as that.'

'Who are you kidding?' she said, laughing. 'I phoned and you came? Robbie, I couldn't count the number of times we phoned you when . . . '

He didn't want to offer any encouragement for her to finish the sentence. Elizabeth had never mastered the family trait of sweeping things under the carpet, but Robbie knew that if he didn't allow the conversation to happen there, in the relative anonymity of the pub, it would find another way out that was ill-timed or inappropriate.

'When what?' he asked, bracing himself.

'When you buggered off down South,' she said, the words slipping quickly off her tongue. 'Mum barely left the house in the hope that the phone would ring and it would be you on the other end, offering an explanation or telling us you were tired of messing around in Dublin and were coming home. But then again, seeing Mum give up hope was worse than the weeks she held on to the thinning belief that you were made of better, stronger stuff. One day she stopped waiting, stopped asking Wendy to ring you, stopped even talking about you.'

A knot was tying itself inside Robbie's stomach, gathering all the stray ends of his good intentions and clumping them together until it was difficult to swallow.

'But then I started phoning, remember? I rang Mum a lot and even you from time to time, birthdays and that – you can't say I didn't.' He was pleading with her, begging for a pardon so that he might leave the conversation feeling better about himself.

Elizabeth had been shaking her head in disbelief and Robbie hated the version of himself they were discussing. He had taken great care to remould himself in Dublin, smoothing the edges where once he was rough and discarding the unwieldy parts of his character. Then he allowed Hannah, his workmates, his in-laws and whoever else breezed through his life, to redress him in hues of Dublin snobbery, journalistic excellence, alcoholic abandon and marital responsibility. He was blended, unmade and remade, rubbed at, primed, challenged and patted on the back until he fitted into their boxes perfectly.

'I've changed, ok, Lizzie? Can't you see that? I'm older now and that past is so far behind me that I can't bear to hear you talk about the person I was then,' Robbie said, knocking back the dregs of his glass for emphasis.

'Well isn't that great for you, Robbie,' she said with glee, loud enough to attract the attention of an older couple sitting next to them. She observed him for a moment, her head bobbing from too much alcohol, and then leant across the table so he could hear her whisper.

'You may have changed, brother, you may be in a different place geographically and emotionally, but we're all still back there in that big farmhouse wondering where you are. Mum's still waiting by the phone, I'm still young and trying not to blame myself, and Wendy's in the process of deciding how hard she needs to be to rescue us all from that bastard we call father.

'We may have moved on in every other aspect of our lives: growing up, finding new love, leaving home, but when we see you, we're all thrust right back there because things have to be resolved to move past them. You made that impossible for us, though, because you were too scared.'

For the time it took Elizabeth to deliver her speech, Robbie had been weighed down as though someone was standing behind him, pressing his shoulders to stop him from moving. Gone were the images he had stored of his younger sister: wide-eyed, innocent and proud of his accomplishments. How would he relate to her now that he had become so reduced in her mind? She watched him for a moment and then stood up from the table, hesitated briefly and walked out the door.

'Can I take this chair, mate?' a man wearing tweed asked only moments after Elizabeth had left.

Robbie nodded. She wasn't coming back.

Eleven

Whether it was guilt or genuine desire that made Robbie buy his mother and two sisters tickets for the garden show was unimportant. Watching them coo and stroke one another's summery clothing comforted him. It was so dazzlingly feminine and made him yearn for his wife. They had spoken on the phone every day since he had left Dublin and Robbie longed to feel as much for her when they were together, as he did apart. All the love, desire and passion he had for her seemed so much stronger and more concentrated in her absence. It meant that he said things and made promises and declarations that he felt were possible when he uttered them but inevitably proved less appealing in reality. Their separation this time was no exception. He repeatedly vocalised his loneliness and need for her while she remained clipped and confident, puffed up with the knowledge that, when forced to, she coped very well on her own. She admitted that to him, not out of spite, but in a way that showed that she was surprised by her own strength.

'Ironic isn't it?' he had said. 'That I come face to face with my inadequacy and you discover you're better off without me.'

It was a cheap ploy but he had just had the showdown with Elizabeth and was desperate for someone to be on his side. Hannah softened and they talked on for over an hour, longer than any conversation they had had for years. When he finished the phone call he was reassured that regardless of the outcome of his trip, he had a family in Dublin to which he would return.

Wendy had arrived with Elizabeth, the two of them dressed in skirts that filled with the wind like yacht sails. Elizabeth was holding the top of an ornate straw hat against Wendy's head to see if it fitted.

'I'm not wearing that,' Wendy said as Robbie went out to meet them. 'A fancy skirt is one thing but I'm not getting ideas above my station.'

Robbie laughed as her statement carried across the driveway.

'We wouldn't want that now, would we?' he said.

Wendy's smile was tight and he wondered if Elizabeth had said anything about their conversation.

'Don't think you're getting away without an accessory,' Elizabeth said, producing a baker boy hat from the back seat, like the one he used to wear as a child.

'Ta da!' she said, presenting it as though no bad words had passed between them. 'I know it's not Ascot but it's the closest we'll get, so put the hats on and let's get over there before the field fills up with cars and we have to walk for miles.'

Hillsborough Castle was tucked behind the small town, so well concealed that one could easily frequent the quaint shops on the street or eat in the coffee shops and restaurants for years without being aware of its existence. Its entrance was gated and Robbie thought it looked more like a government building than the gatehouse to extensive grounds and an eighteenth-century manor.

'I never knew there was so much ground back here,' Elizabeth said, her heeled shoes clipping like fingers on a keyboard as they followed the walkway to the walled garden.

'It's a lovely day,' Robbie said and the three hummed their agreement, turning their faces towards the sun.

When we see you, we're all thrust right back there. Elizabeth's words were on repeat in his mind. He regarded them swinging their hips and muttering to one another about smells and trees and the sunlight; the three women who shared in his growing up and then failed to understand what they had produced. He remembered Wendy, younger and permed, on the doorstep of his bedsit in Belfast, making demands of him and almost crying with frustration. It was her first time in the city; Elizabeth had instructed her on what bus to take and where he lived, and Robbie knew the anxiety it must have caused her to be there that day. The light had been dirty and dim in the room. She had refused a drink and was content to stand until Robbie cleared a space for her on his bed.

'When we said journalism, we didn't mean this kind of journalism,' Wendy had said. She described it as pointless, dangerous and even seedy. Their mother had read the kind of 'dirt' he had been 'digging up' about 'paramilitary scum'. It was when she told him that their parents were ashamed that he threw her out onto the then-dark street and relished the fear she would feel groping about for the bus station.

He bumped into a man walking towards him and his mother linked her arm with his.

'You're very deep in thought,' she said.

'I've got a lot on my mind.'

'I'm sure you're missing your family. It's so hard to be separated from them.'

Robbie met her eye.

They walked on in silence, the clamour and fuss of the show growing louder as they neared the walled garden. *Plant a seed, grow a dream* was the tag line for the weekend and every available space was testament to how seriously the exhibitors took their mission. Stalls selling everything from sweet pea to rare varieties of rose lined the castle wall, with more on the lawn offering home-made produce. His sisters were giddy as they tasted unusual preserves, barbequed meat and cupcakes loaded with icing while deliberating about what to buy.

80

If Robbie had been less inclined to wander off on his own, he might have avoided her, or at least seen her and given himself the choice of approaching her or not. But, as it happened, they had both chosen to seek sanctuary in the deserted bandstand on the outskirts of the gardens. He had seen it from afar; its shade promised a moment's solitude and an opportunity to observe passersby from a distance. It was a habit that had led him to journalism, the very occupation that allowed him to scoop so many exclusive stories. He would set himself up in a pub/park/street corner and sit or stand quietly until he was as invisible as the barstool he sat on, or the wall he leant against. Things would happen around him, people would forget to lower their voices and no one suspected the fresh-faced lad he was then.

Nothing could have prepared him to see Martin's wife, all six foot of her folded onto one of the low walls in between the pillars. He had paraded into the bandstand, thinking himself alone and had stumbled across her before it was too late to retrace his steps. They considered one another briefly before looking away and then back again immediately.

'Joan?' he said, hand against his chest as though the sight of her had stolen his breath.

For a moment, she didn't respond but sat staring at him quizzically. He could tell that she recognised him but was weighing something up in her mind.

'Robbie Hanright, well I never,' she said eventually, standing up. 'You think you get to a point in life where little surprises you but . . . '

'My mother and sisters are out there somewhere sniffing at flowers. I thought I'd escape for a while.'

'I'm doing something similar myself,' she said.

She had aged considerably since their last meeting five years before. Her once prominent and striking cheekbones were draped with skin that had long since lost its elasticity and no attempt had been made to cover the sprigs of grey highlighting her shoulder-length brown hair. However, it was her eyes that had changed the most. They no longer danced with mischief; they were duller and half-shut against the world, with eyelids that sagged like ankle socks and untamed, bushy brows.

'You've changed,' she said and took a cigarette from the packet in her hand. 'There must be someone looking after you by the look of that gut.'

He dropped his head.

'I'm married now, got a little girl who's only six months old.' It was said like an apology.

'You didn't marry a Dub, did you?' she said.

'I suppose I did,' he said, looking about him in embarrassment.

'Very good.'

'What about you?'

'Oh, you know, just plodding along as usual. The kids are good. Mary has just started the Academy, and Abbey is still in Primary.'

Robbie thought of Knockbracken Hospital with its squeaky linoleum and wards that smelt of disinfectant and despair. Joan had seemed out of place there and did not want to stay but she had been sectioned when the police found her sitting alone in her Vauxhall Astra with a length of hose pipe in her car boot. That was the last time Robbie had seen her, curled on the bed like a cat. He had watched her a while and felt the ache of their shared grief so completely that it nearly knocked him over. Their conversation was mostly one-sided; she was angry that he had not stopped the doctor from forcing her to stay and although he was there to say goodbye, to list all the reasons he had to move away, Robbie could not bring himself to face it and he left the hospital thinking he would never see her again. He wrote a letter a month later. It was full of guilt-infused justifications that he knew she would have hated. *Sorry for deserting you, but I . . .*

'What brings you to these parts? I suppose you're up and down all the time with that fancy new road?' she said, drawing hard on her cigarette.

'Not exactly. This is my first time back in five years.'

'You're not serious?' she said and then gave a short, sarcastic laugh when he nodded. 'I'd say there's been a fair bit of grovelling then, am I right?'

'Something like that.'

'What are you working at now then?' she said, changing the subject.

'I write for the culture section of a Dublin newspaper.'

'That's a bit of a step down.'

'It's not that bad, getting paid to sit in the theatre or cinema or whatever big thing is going on in the city. Dublin's a different world.'

She screwed up her nose. 'It's not for me. I hated living in Monaghan, so boring and uneventful and I never really felt like we fitted in.'

'You would love Dublin; it's full of life. You're always meeting people and trying new things.'

'Life changes when you don't have someone to do those things with,' she said quietly. 'Just me and the girls now. They're all the life I need. There's a quare lot of energy that goes in to raising little ones, just you wait and see.'

They laughed then and for a moment Robbie could believe they were old friends passing the time of day.

'I'd better get back,' Joan said, standing and grinding her cigarette butt into the cement floor.

'Yeah, me too. Great bumping into you, Joan.'

They were standing face to face, he with his hands shoved into his pockets and she with a look of expectation that Robbie might say something else. There were many things running through his head, but they would open something between them that he was content to keep shut. *Sorry for deserting you.*

She pursed her lips and waved before walking away. Her elasticised jeans were too short in the leg and revealed blue and white polka-dot socks. After using his shirtsleeve to wipe the sweat from his forehead, Robbie strode off in the opposite direction.

Twelve

Robbie woke feeling impatient, as if the day stretching before him did not contain enough hours for the things he needed to do. And yet what needed to be done was so indistinct – more like vague shapes and feelings than anything solid that he could write on a list.

It was the end of the week and he was beginning to feel as though his reason for being there was less clear in his mind than it had been when he arrived. As the morning grew behind the curtains, he felt a sudden impatience to return to Dublin, to a place where he knew the boundaries and limitations of his relationships, where there was routine and fewer expectations and where he knew himself better in relation to the people and things around him. He was far from home in the messy room he had inhabited all week. Even the clothes that were hung over chairs and discarded on the floor seemed foreign and out of place, and his family's initial welcome was beginning to give way to frayed tempers.

The impulse to cross the border was so appealing that he almost got out of bed with the intention of throwing everything in a suitcase and leaving before the house woke up but something kept him beneath his duvet. *Things have to be resolved to move past them.* Life moved too quickly for Robbie to lie in bed and consider such statements. Awake before dawn most mornings, he had a child to dress, a twenty-minute walk to the

Luas, a crammed commute and a staff meeting to attend every morning. It was not possible to have emotional setbacks on the way to the top; he had seen one too many colleagues trampled by keener, younger journalists while they wallowed in divorced stupors or mid-life crises. In the newsroom, if you did not pick yourself up and keep moving, someone would stand on you on their way out the door to cover your story.

It was on his twenty-first birthday that Robbie got a call from Martin. It was a Friday afternoon and most of his colleagues had left the office. The thought of a bus ride to Dromore to spend his birthday with his family kept him behind, digging through paperwork to find things to do. Martin's voice was strained and loud against the background noise.

'O'Keegan here, I can't talk for long. Take the six o'clock train to Dundalk. I'll be waiting for you there.'

Robbie hadn't even hesitated. The moment Martin hung up, he was on his feet, gathering his bits and pieces and making for the door. He had been working with his elder for several years at that stage but had seen little of the action that had earned Martin his reputation. The majority of their conversations took place on the phone when Martin gave Robbie orders and dictated facts that he wanted his assistant to work into a story. People spoke about Martin as though he were a phantom, or an elusive hound, hot on the heels of paramilitary scandal, but Robbie was beginning to doubt whether he would ever leave his desk in the newsroom to join him.

The whole journey on the train was spent wondering what Martin could possibly want him for. He was part terrified, part curious and by the time he stepped on to the platform, into a wind so strong he felt as though he was being slapped, he was giddy with anticipation. Martin approached him and steered him towards the exit where a car was waiting. They drove in silence until he parked at the very back of a huge industrial car park.

'I won't beat around the bush, Robbie. Me and the wife had to leave Lurgan. I'll be living in Monaghan for . . . well I don't know how long – as long as it takes. So I need someone on the ground to go where I say, when I say. I can't give you any more details. If you know, you can tell, d'ya understand?'

The next thing Martin handed him a cell phone and his car keys and told him to wait for his call. Robbie noticed only then that there was another car parked in the opposite corner of the car park that had turned on its lights and started driving towards them. There was a woman behind the wheel whom he later got to know as Joan and then suddenly Martin was gone and Robbie was in the car alone on the outskirts of Dundalk.

That night, as he drove back across the border, his hands shook and his mind raced to keep up with the direction his life might be taking. The thing he had always wanted was suddenly happening and the reality of it was much more frightening than he had imagined. He had been attracted to journalism because the idea of being out and about with a notepad appealed to him. Seeing his name in print and introducing himself as a journalist were only two of the egocentric reasons he had coveted the career and when he was finally given a chance to walk in his idol's shoes, he started to worry that they might not fit.

He rolled over in the bed and sighed, remembering the quiet kitchen that night he had returned home. A half-eaten cake sat on the table, its crumbs strewn about the place like scattered seed. The dishes were stacked on the draining board; there had been at least twenty people in the house that night to celebrate his birthday. His mother did not speak to him the next morning, Wendy took her gift back to the shop and Robbie was too guilty to even apologise. *Things have to be resolved to move past them.*

₭

Wendy's car was in the driveway of the farmhouse when Robbie arrived. Its boot was open and full of orange, plastic shopping bags, flapping in the wind. Wendy came out of the house, gave Robbie a nod of acknowledgement and began gathering the shopping.

'You're not supposed to be driving,' she said.

'I'm managing ok.'

'It's not safe. Six weeks, isn't that what they told you?'

She had been talking to Margaret.

'That's right but I'm fine, really. Let me help you,' Robbie said, locking his car and lifting bags with his left hand.

'What are you doing here?' Wendy asked, hooking the bags onto her wrists.

'I'm taking Dad to the hospital.'

Wendy stopped to look at him.

'What?'

'He's going in for his whipples procedure today. Didn't he tell you?' Robbie said, swallowing hard.

'Unbelievable,' she muttered, gathering the last two bags in haste.

'Wendy, wait. Don't be angry, he probably didn't want to worry you. It's nothing to get upset about.'

'Why didn't he ask *me*?'

'I don't know. I don't have much else to do and I offered to take him.'

She set the bags on the tarmac, closed the boot and made for the driver's seat.

'Wendy, don't go. Please.'

'I wasn't stopping anyway. Steven is selling sheep tonight and needs some help with the tagging.'

She paused by the car door. 'Will you phone me?'

'Of course.'

With that, she reversed out of the driveway and left.

'Is Wendy away?' his father said when Robbie appeared in the kitchen with the shopping. He was sitting at the table poking a screwdriver into the back of what looked like a battery-powered radio.

'Yes. She had to go on – something about selling sheep.'

His father did not look up. Robbie put the groceries into cupboards, all the while watching his father – spectacles balanced on the end of his nose and fingers too large and clumsy for the job. Eventually he gave a satisfied grunt and turned a dial on the front of the radio. Loud pop music sang into the kitchen, startling them. John twisted another knob until the volume was lower and classical music replaced the teenage riffs.

'For the hospital,' he explained.

'You could use my iPod. It's much handier to transport than that old thing.'

His father swatted at his suggestion and stood up from the table.

'This will do,' he said. 'I've got a few things to throw into my bag and then we'll be on our way.'

Robbie checked his watch.

'Don't be long, Dad.'

While waiting for his father, Robbie went for a walk around the back of the house. The yard that was once scrubbed clean to show the white cement was now grey from run-off dirt from the greenhouses. Beyond the dilapidated pig houses Robbie could see the orchard thick with fruit trees and the sun piercing them as though finding chinks in their armour. Nettles as tall as a man had grown between the trees, their wide hairy leaves reminding Robbie of childhood stings made better by dock plants. It always amazed him that the cure grew in such close proximity to the thing that caused the ailment in the first place. The thick brown chimney pot that his mother had dug into the ground all those years ago was still there. It had weathered the storms, despite his father's protestation that it would fall to pieces with the first bout of heavy rain. The miniature rose bush that she had planted as a seedling was now blooming confidently from the pot, its wide-open apricot flowers providing the only colour in the orchard.

Somewhere beneath the unkempt vegetation Robbie could visualise Elizabeth tucked in the shade of one of the trees reading a book. He could see his father, younger and more capable, turning over piles of pig manure to allow it to dry in the sun. Wendy would be trying to help him, loitering awkwardly at his elbow until shooed away or ignored long enough to infuriate her. Then she would turn to Robbie and start interfering with whatever game he was playing until she had ruined it or lost her temper trying to change the rules. It was harder to place his mother. She was mostly removed from the picture, working indoors to keep things ticking over so there would be food on the table and clean clothes in their wardrobes. Robbie sighed. What kind of a life did she have?

He could hear his father calling him from the house. The chickens appeared from one of the greenhouses at the sound of his voice and came running down the yard behind Robbie.

'What are you at up there?' he asked Robbie.

'Just walking around the orchard.'

His father gave a short, sharp laugh.

'It's a jungle, isn't it? Hasn't seen a strimmer in years.'

'Why didn't you ever get someone to do it for you?'

His father looked at him, as though the answer to his question was too obvious to warrant a response.

'Like who, son?'

'I don't know. You can pay for that kind of thing,' Robbie said, pushing past his father. 'We'd better go, Dad. We'll be late otherwise.'

His father was silent until they were within sight of the hospital. The building loomed tall and offensive on the Belfast skyline, visible from most parts of the city.

'How's your mother?' his father asked him.

'Fine, I think. I didn't get to see her this morning.'

'And your sisters?'

'Dad, you know as well as I do.'

'But I'm asking how you find them.'

'Oh, fine.'

'Do you mind the time we kept ducks?' his father said, twiddling his thumbs in his lap.

'Vaguely, I was very young.'

'It was your mother wanted them. She heard about a boy out near Markethill who was looking to get rid of a few because the fox had been at them. We traipsed over there one afternoon and got six ducks and a goose, all different types; he was selling them together so we had to take them all. Anyway, they were your mother's favourites. You don't remember them, really?'

Robbie shook his head, reluctant to interrupt his father's train of thought. They were pulling into the hospital car park.

'She had little to do with the rest of them. The chickens were a nuisance, the sheep prone to wander and the pigs, well, none of us much liked the pigs.'

Robbie laughed.

'The birds were as wild as they come when we got them, so we clipped their wings. After a few weeks Margaret had them tamed.' He shook his head. 'They'd come down into the yard at the sound of her voice, looking to be fed. She'd throw them some seed or bread or whatever she had and just watch them. Sometimes she'd stand there for a good half hour.'

Robbie turned off the engine and surreptitiously checked his watch.

'One night she came in to me saying the Khaki Campbell was gone. It was going on dark and a duck out roaming at dusk is as good as dead. She searched high and low for it but it was nowhere to be seen. She even took the torch and set out across the fields on her own; it was as if one of you had got lost.'

'Tell me the rest while we walk, Dad,' Robbie said, opening his car door and hurrying round to assist his father. They walked in silence until they had left the car park.

'Must have been three weeks later she came back,' his father said, laughing gently as they passed through the hospital doors.

'What?'

'Aye, the duck came back with six little ones trailing behind her. Never did I see Margaret so happy.'

Robbie watched his father out of the corner of his eye. His head was bowed by the memory and his hands sunk deep into his pockets.

The lift pinged and opened its doors to deliver them onto the oncology ward. Robbie wanted to take his father by the arm, but he moved too slowly and his father had presented himself at reception before Robbie could do anything to reassure him.

Thirteen

The procedure was scheduled for the next morning. When Robbie asked about visiting times, he was told to phone the hospital first but he could possibly see him in the afternoon. Unable to wait, Robbie travelled to Belfast at lunchtime. As he parked in a housing area off the Lisburn Road, Robbie realised that it wasn't the usual feeling of guilt that had motivated his overeager arrival, it was fear. Robbie was scared. He had the same nervous energy he had experienced as a child and later as a husband and father. What if his father died and he had no opportunity to change the way he felt about him?

Robbie had lived most of his life one step ahead of himself, ever since primary school when he was moved up a year for being too smart. At the age of sixteen, his friends were driving cars. He bought a moped, refusing to be left behind. There was always a girl on the go. Not in a throwaway date-her-for-a-week kind of way but always serious, intense and committed. Now, as he walked through the streets and clouds knitted together overhead, he wanted to slow it all down. If only he could rewind to the time before his father was sick so there would never be any doubt of his motivation.

Martin had been taken to the Royal Hospital. Robbie could remember what Joan had said word for word: 'Martin's been shot. We're going to the Royal. I just want to say that if you knew about this, I swear to God I'll never forgive you'.

Memories of driving at top speed along every back road and short cut he knew stayed with him as he walked down the Lisburn Road into the city centre. He knew the country roads of Armagh like the back of his hand. Their sharp corners, unexpected endings, dips and troughs were so familiar that even as he walked the streets of Belfast, he could still retrace his drive, distracting his mind by considering other routes that might have delivered him at the hospital a minute sooner. If he had not wasted those precious minutes behind a silage-heavy tractor, he might have got there in time to speak to Martin, say his goodbyes, explain the way things had happened. Instead, he met Joan in the hallway, five minutes too late.

'He asked for you,' she said.

He would never know what Martin wanted to say. Robbie liked to think that he would have understood; that something of the deeper nature of what they had signed up for would be kindred between them. That was what he chose to believe, until time passed and the significance of words on paper started to diminish in his mind.

He stepped into a newsagent to buy cigarettes. It was four years since he had smoked but there was something unsettling about walking through such familiar territory. On the way out of the shop, he stopped at the newspaper section. There was a time when the very smell of newsprint would give him an adrenaline rush. The stories had power; they unearthed scandals and things done in secret. Society depended on them for information and enlightenment and Robbie was an integral part of it all. He scanned the headlines. *Jobs under threat as Coffee Republic goes bust*; *Set for a scorcher as climate change ignored*; *The death of a King, memorial in LA*; *Cat shot in the eye in Holy Lands*. His old newspaper was as bright and trashy as he remembered. SOME NECK: *How vicious thugs Wayne Dundon and 'Lex Looter' want to silence us* by Mark Wilson. The heading made him shiver. He left the shop and lit a cigarette on its doorstep. He remembered how it felt to write such damning reports on a daily basis. The metallic taste of fear at seeing his own stories in print was impossible to forget. Did Mark Wilson lie awake in bed at night too, savouring the thought of how close he lived to danger? Did it wake him up in the morning, full of energy, raring to go? Or was he older, with a wife and kids? Did he want out because he had started to count the cost and it was not worth it?

It began to rain. Robbie turned up the collar of his jacket and shielded his cigarette in the palm of his hand to stop it from getting wet. It took his mind off things to walk through the rain, avoiding the sharp ends of umbrella spokes and thinking about where he might go. Belfast looked more like itself when it was wet: dark, ominous and full of people in a rush to get somewhere. He thought of his father laid out on the operating table. When it was over, he wouldn't be cured; he would just live a bit longer and feel less pain when he died. What would it feel like to be fatherless? He would refer to his father in the past tense, with the kind of retrospective rosiness that forbade people to speak ill of the dead. Apart from that, little would change. He would still never see or talk to him and the past would be solidified and unchangeable.

Three CDs for a Fiver, the sign read. Robbie went into the music store, drawn by a bargain. The shop was a popular place for people to find sanctuary from the rain. It smelt like soggy trainers and he tried his best to avoid rubbing shoulders with the rest of the drenched customers browsing alongside him. As usual, the promise of a sale held little reward. It was an excuse to dig out everything unsellable from their stockroom and dupe customers into buying it. Robbie could not stand the steamy huddle in the sale section and headed for the back of the shop where the old vinyl records were kept. It was empty apart from one other customer, and an open window diffused the smell from the front of the shop. As Robbie thumbed his way through a collection of 1970s' LPs, he spotted the familiar, bright yellow jacket of a Bob Dylan record. As he turned the record over and scanned the track list, he became aware of someone standing close by. The girl he had noticed when he started looking in that section was now at his right shoulder staring at the LP enviously.

She blew her fringe from her eyes and reached over to touch the record sleeve.

'The poor immigrant with tears like the rain,' she said quietly, smiling. 'Great album.'

Robbie stood still for several minutes after she had left the shop, the chorus playing in his mind and every word of the song as clear to him as if he had listened to it only that morning. In truth it had probably been twenty years since he had heard it. Why of all the songs that crackled through their living room was that the one that stayed with him? For a brief moment he was immersed: the deep sense of sadness the lyrics evoked and the memory of walking into the living room as a young boy, long after bedtime, to see his parents hand in hand on the sofa with their eyes closed to appreciate the third and final verse. Whose visions in the final end must shatter like the glass. He took the record to the till and paid for it.

∞

Robbie was so relieved to find his sisters in the hospital waiting room that he hugged them each for several seconds. Unsure as to how to respond, they turned the conversation to their father.

'The doctor said it went well,' Elizabeth assured him. 'We'll be able to see him soon.'

Robbie took a seat opposite them and started to yawn. Having his sisters there instantly relieved the pressure he had been feeling. With a ban on fresh flowers in the hospital wards, they came with plastic ones to brighten the room and things for their father to read and eat. Wendy knew to bring pyjamas and had packed the belongings neatly into plastic bags that sat at her feet.

They knew their father – what he ate, read and would feel comfortable in. There was a confidence in them being there that he did not feel. The language for discussing his illness and care was familiar to them and he felt as though he was merely being tolerated, just because he had come all that way, just because their father was dying.

'Robert Hanright?' a woman in light blue scrubs asked the waiting room.

Robbie looked at his sisters, who ushered him ahead of them.

His father was tubed and tired. There were dark rings around his eyes and his veined hands were twitching by his side. The room was bare, with a window overlooking the Lisburn Road and all the students it housed walking to and fro.

'I brought you a few necessities and some treats,' Wendy said, clipped and professional. 'You'll be in for a night at least but there are two pairs of pyjamas here just in case.'

She laid the items on the bed as she listed them. Robbie and Elizabeth stood back until she had finished and John regarded her with suspicion.

'I wasn't sure now what you'd prefer to read. I found this.' She held up the *Buy and Sell* newspaper. 'I know you like to look through this and it was out today. There's also a few back issues of *Farmers Weekly* that Steven had lying about. I had a flick through them and there are a few good stories in there about calving that . . .'

Their father was waving his hand in her direction, barely able to lift his arm off the bed. Wendy stopped talking and made a sound like a hiccup. She dropped her head, made as if to reach for her father's hand but then stopped herself and started to cry. Robbie looked at Elizabeth, who turned on him with tears in her eyes. It was as if the soles of his shoes had melted into the floor. His father looked at him.

'I brought you something too,' Robbie said.

The girls turned, their crying stunted. Robbie removed the

record from the black HMV bag and held it up for his father to see.

'I found it hiding away in the record section in town. Thought you'd like it.'

Wendy stood up from where she had been balancing on the edge of her father's bed, Elizabeth moved in to study the sleeve and his father removed his hand from Wendy's to reach for the album. His lips were shaking and Robbie looked away.

'Well,' Elizabeth said, exhaling loudly. 'Tell you what, Dad. We'll grab some coffee while the nurse sorts you out. You're moving to the ward shortly, so we'll come and see you there.'

She didn't wait for a response before leading Robbie by the arm towards the door. They waited for Wendy outside. No one spoke as they followed the signs towards the cafeteria.

'You wouldn't know what time of the day it was,' Elizabeth remarked as they stood in the queue. The other two looked around them, registering the neon-lit refectory with its garish, red plastic chairs. Hot metal slabs kept the remains of a lasagne and a few slices of dried up chicken pie warm. The smell turned Robbie's stomach.

'Have you eaten?' Wendy asked.

Robbie shook his head.

'Pity there wasn't something a bit more appealing,' she said, using a salad spoon to poke the yellow coleslaw.

With coffees in hand, the siblings took a table in the back corner of the room. Young doctors and nurses chatted around them in small groups.

'He looks like shit,' Elizabeth said.

'Lizzie,' Wendy scolded, 'what did you expect?'

'I don't know.' Elizabeth stared into her paper cup.

'What did you imagine Dad would do with that record?' Wendy asked, meeting Robbie's eye with a cold, determined stare. The question took him off guard. He had just been considering the moment in the room that was so charged with emotion. He had never experienced anything like that with his family and he had the distinct impression that Wendy was about to undermine it.

'I realise that it's not as practical as pyjamas or as useful as reading material but I just saw it and thought of him. It wasn't really planned.'

'Well, if you want my opinion,' she snapped, folding her arms, 'I thought it was an ill-timed gift.'

'Please don't fight,' Elizabeth said.

'Why is that?' Robbie asked, ignoring Elizabeth.

'Bringing up the past when he's vulnerable isn't good for him.'

'Maybe it's good for him to remember the good times. What's wrong with that?'

He gulped the lukewarm coffee and started to rip little pieces off the polystyrene rim.

'There's just no point. It was so long ago and a lot has happened since then.'

'He and Mum loved that record.'

'I don't remember it,' Elizabeth interjected.

'The two of them used to sit up listening to it; it was a long time ago, maybe, but a happy time all the same,' Robbie said.

Wendy sighed. 'Sometimes they danced,' she said.

All three were quiet as the canteen filled up around them.

'What are we going to do?' Wendy said. 'I'd take him in but we just don't have the space.'

'You know he would never leave the farm,' Robbie said.

'Well, he might not have much of a choice.'

'It's not an option, Wendy. He'd rather die.'

'And you know that, do you?'

Robbie ripped the polystyrene into thin shreds.

'Stop it,' Elizabeth said. Two nurses at an adjacent table turned to look at them. 'For God's sake, you two. Could you give over for long enough for us to have a sensible conversation about this?'

'Sorry, Lizzie,' Robbie said, reaching for her hand. 'All I'm saying is that I think we should try and think of something that allows him to stay in the house.'

'Are you offering to move in with him?' Lizzie said, laughing.

Robbie stared at his fingers.

'Well . . .'

'Oh come on, your life is in Dublin now,' Wendy said.

'I have some time,' he said, looking between his sisters.

'It's the best we can do at the moment,' Wendy said, sweeping into her hand the bits of cup that Robbie had discarded. She stood up to deposit them in the bin and he noticed how much she had let herself go. Her hair, once styled and glossy, was scraped off her face and secured with a velvet ruffle. Nothing she wore gave any hint of her body's shape and a jumper hung asymmetrically from her armpits. Her hands were the only part of her that looked feminine, but even they seemed awkward when she walked. When she returned to the table, she hovered self-consciously, suggesting that they go up to the ward. Robbie and Elizabeth linked arms and followed her to the elevator.

Fourteen

Unpacking his things in his old bedroom, Robbie was struck by how much smaller it seemed. The roof was closer to his head and the space that the desk demanded seemed farcical, but it was warm and cosy, unlike the large room he had occupied in his mother's house.

Because the front door extended out from the house, there was a small stone ledge beneath Robbie's bedroom window where he used to sit on summer evenings to look over the garden. As a child he believed it to be his ledge. Neither of his sisters was allowed onto it, but then neither was he after he tried to jump off it into the driveway. After that his mother had painted the sash windows shut so that not only was he forbidden access to his secret ledge, he had to keep his bedroom door ajar to let in the air.

Palette knife in hand, he set about loosening the window from its frame. Strips of dried paint fell onto the carpet as he worked the knife in the joints. Twenty minutes later, after exerting a lot of energy to coax the window upwards one-handed, a fresh gust of air ballooned the curtains and unsettled the dust in the room. His mother had, wisely, given him a plastic bag of cleaning products.

'If I know your father at all, he won't have lifted a finger to tidy that place. Wendy does odds and ends but she'll never have touched your room,' she told him.

As he cleaned, he wondered what his father would make of him settling into his old bedroom. The siblings had decided not to tell him, so as not to upset him when he needed his strength. The operation designed to improve his situation had in fact worsened it.

'It's quite common,' the doctor had said, 'especially in elderly people who have kept themselves busy to avoid thinking about their illness.'

Robbie wanted to punch the doctor. If it was such a common occurrence, why had no one warned them?

It was decided that Robbie would stay at the house and tend to the animals until his father had regained his strength. Neither Robbie nor his sisters believed that their father would ever recover sufficiently to run what was left of the farm but they were not ready to admit it. The last remaining cow needed to be milked twice a day and Robbie could not fathom why his father insisted on keeping the animal when the milk went to waste and it got him out of bed at five o'clock in the morning. The chickens took care of themselves and with the grass growing at such a rate, the sheep would no longer need hay to supplement their feed. The thought of sitting beneath the swollen udder of a cow before the sun had even roused itself filled Robbie with dread, but he settled himself with the thought that he would be doing something useful.

After polishing the desk and changing the bed linen, Robbie sneezed his way through the vacuuming. Wendy would be arriving the next morning with their father, and Robbie wanted to move John's bedroom downstairs, give the kitchen a going over and sort the animals out before it got dark. He could hear the rooster crowing in the yard, its croaky warble misplaced in the mid-afternoon.

As a child, Robbie had imagined living in the farmhouse when he was older. The fields with holes in their hedges and stiles to climb over used to take him deep into the countryside where rivers were overgrown with brambles and badgers dug their holes. On bright winter days his mother would make sure he wrapped up warm before sending him out to pick sloe berries with his sisters or to help Mr. Murray bang metal buckets of feed to bring the cows in for milking. When he returned at dusk, the living room was always warm from the open peat fire and his mother was occupied and content in the adjacent kitchen. As he moved into his teenage years, the appeal of living on a farm wore off. The rooms became claustrophobic and conversations stilted, the chores were mundane and he was more interested in television than exploring the countryside around him.

Larkscroft Farm had been built by his great-grandfather in the 1800s. Back then it would have been the only property in the area, the rest of the houses at the crossroads having been built in the last fifty years. A weathered black and white photograph on the wall of the living room showed two plump individuals, his great-grandmother and great-grandfather, standing to attention against the pebble-dashed wall of their new farmhouse. The sash windows were bright white and the glass so clean that it was possible to see all the way through the living room and kitchen to the backyard. The barns and outhouses were built later, by Robbie's father's father. He had kept pigs and built two long houses roofed with sheets of galvanised tin. John had many stories of mucking out the sheds as a boy in the summertime. His cousins would have come to lend a hand, each taking two sheds and competing to clean theirs the best. The stench had put him off pig farming for life.

It wasn't until John inherited the house that a second storey was constructed. He and Margaret's brothers built it brick by brick, elevating the roof on posts as they went. Robbie was a toddler then and had only vague memories of shirtless men on the rooftops and lots of banging. It meant that John and Margaret's bedroom was moved upstairs and two additional rooms slept Robbie and his sisters. What was once his parents' bedroom became the good room, where it was always too cold for visitors to remove their coats when they called over for tea. Over the years fewer and fewer people came and it eventually became a storage room that Margaret nicknamed Narnia.

The greenhouses were erected when Robbie was six. He remembered the panes of glass being slotted in like Connect Four pieces and the neat rows of things that his father had growing within months. There were three of them, each one elevated above the other as though they were on steps. A complicated watering system was laid beneath the soil and the trees around the periphery cut down to allow maximum light to reach the plants. On cold days Robbie would often close himself inside the glasshouse and enjoy the steamy breath of the soil and the thick smell of ripening fruit. When he first learnt the word 'sanctuary', he often pictured the greenhouse at the top of the garden where a grapevine grew along the roof and it was possible to hide among its boughs and feel safe. Even now the word brought the same image to mind.

Robbie switched off the vacuum cleaner and looked at the sign in the front garden advertising the exclusive development that would some day wipe out any shred of the generations of memories invested in the farmhouse.

The greenhouses were no longer hot houses full of fruit and vegetables; they were dilapidated and overrun with weeds. Only that morning Wendy had made a note in her diary to phone about getting them torn down. She called it a health and safety issue and said she could not let her boys outside if it stayed the way it was. The tin roofs of the pig sheds had rusted through in places and great slabs of asbestos were piled outside them to block the entrances. Even the house itself was a shell of what his relatives had once built. What would his great-grandfather make of it all? The bathroom roof had not been sealed for years and mould grew thick and black across the ceiling and down the walls. Very little money had been spent to ensure that the house kept up with the times. Every suggestion that Margaret had made of replacing peeling wallpaper or threadbare carpets was shot down and she was reduced to moving the furniture to cover the worst parts of the wear. Robbie cast his eye over the bedroom before wheeling in his suitcase. The open window let in the heavy smell of peat smoke; someone in the district had lit a fire.

℁

The next morning Wendy's car pulled in as Robbie was getting out of the bath. He swore and gathered his towel around him to let her in.

'You're early,' he called to her. She turned, observed him, shook her head and looked away.

Robbie left her negotiating a wheelchair from the boot and went upstairs to put on some clothes. Despite the promise of summer, he had woken that morning to a cold house and, after wrapping up in his father's old cardigans, most of which smelt of slurry and musty trainers, he discovered that the oil tank was empty. He spent a small fortune on emergency oil from the 24-hour garage and ordered two hundred litres over the phone as soon as County Down Oil offices opened.

As he pulled on his clothes, he looked out of his window to watch Wendy trying to help their father out of the passenger seat, all the while ignoring a litany of abuse. Robbie pitied her. She had all the things she had spent a lifetime looking for – a husband, a house, children and a solid job – but her unhappiness was palpable. He wished she would just let out all the frustration and disappointment she harboured. If only she would say the things she had stored up instead of allowing them to implode, maybe it would be easier to like her.

'Morning, Father,' Robbie said when he came down the stairs.

'What's going on? Why are you in my house?' John tried not to lean on Wendy as he came through the door.

'Come in here and sit down. We'll have a cup of tea and fill you in,' Wendy said, trying to steer him towards the living room.

'This smells like a bloody mutiny,' he said. 'And I'm telling you right now, I won't be having any of it. I'm perfectly able to look after myself.'

Wendy and Robbie said nothing as he leant against the wall for a moment before signalling for the wheelchair to take him into the living room.

By the time Wendy had boiled the kettle and made a pot of tea, their father looked heavy-eyed in his chair. Robbie motioned to her that they take their cups outside and leave him to sleep.

'It'll take him a few days to realise he's not as ok as he likes to think he is,' Robbie said in the yard.

'Do you remember when you made this?' Wendy said, rubbing her hand over the rough wood of the picnic bench on which they were sitting.

'I left Dad's tools sitting out and they were nicked, that's the abiding memory for me I'm afraid.'

Wendy laughed.

'You and Dad spent so much time working away at it, just the two of you.'

'Did we?'

'You don't remember?'

He shook his head.

'I do,' she said. 'It took you the best part of a weekend to measure and cut and nail it all together. After you left, Dad had it up in the orchard. Most nights I'd find him up there, just sitting between the crab apple trees, drinking from that dirty old hip flask of his. That was how he passed his evenings. Even when Joe or that old farmer from the place on the corner down there, what was his name . . .'

'Woods,' Robbie said. 'Sammy Woods.'

'Yes, that's it. Even when they called in, they were straight through the shed and up to the orchard to see him.'

Robbie stared into his teacup.

'It's just a bench,' he said.

She sighed.

The day was sunny but crisp with the tail end of a flight path streaked across the sky. A house martin landed on the end of the table and Robbie noticed how rough and unfinished the edges were. The wood had come from an old house that was being knocked down on their road. John took the wheelbarrow up the hill and returned with several planks of oak that had once been a porch roof. Robbie was summoned into the yard to record measurements and hold the wood while his father sawed it to the correct length. The tools being stolen later that night and the punishment that followed had coloured the day of construction in Robbie's mind but seeing it through Wendy's eyes unsettled him. An image of his father sitting in the orchard on the sagging seats of a picnic bench thinking of him was something he would quite like to believe. A more likely explanation was that he was happier away from his family and his choice of seat was irrelevant. Whether a bar stool or the splintered wood of a picnic bench, the important thing was that he was out of the way and glad to be so.

'What?' Wendy said, swilling the dregs of her tea round her cup. 'You just sighed.'

'Did I? Sorry, it's just difficult for me to imagine Dad like that.'

'Like what?'

'You know, sitting thinking about me.'

Wendy was staring at him. 'You're the prodigal son.'

'What do you mean?'

'Well, neither Lizzie nor I were ever going to run this place,' she said, sweeping her arm about the yard. 'You were the next in line, the farmer-to-be, the prodigal who was faffing around in the city but would some day return. Only you didn't.'

'That's ridiculous,' Robbie said, turning his face towards the sun.

'Is it?'

'Yes. I don't know where you get all this stuff, Wendy, but you need to let it go.'

His sister laughed, stood up and stretched like a cat waking from a nap.

'Whatever you think. I'm going in to check on Dad.'

Robbie waited a while in the yard, scuffing his toes on the cement until he heard the oil tanker on the road. He opened the huge gate that his father had constructed after the theft of his tools and watched the truck reverse into the yard.

Back in the living room, Wendy had heated her father some soup and was tidying around him as he ate. With each mouthful he consumed, he scowled and she rubbed polish into the table even harder. The tension in the room was thick and Robbie turned back to the kitchen to pour a glass of water before joining them.

'Is anyone going to tell me what the bloody hell he's doing here?' he heard his father say.

'It's the animals, Dad . . .' Wendy began.

'It's quite simple,' Robbie said, taking a seat opposite his father. 'The doctor said you need to rest. Resting does not include looking after a farm full of animals.'

'Don't be ridiculous. A handful of chickens, a cow and a few sheep is hardly a farm full. And what good are you anyway with that thing on your arm?'

'Don't you worry about that. You need a hand and I've got at least one I can lend.'

'Sure you're only round the corner with your mother. You don't need to be moving in like this. I never said you could.'

Robbie looked at Wendy.

'Robbie is heading back to Dublin soon, Dad; he thought

you'd like the company until you're a hundred per cent again.'

John grunted.

'Well it's not at all necessary but whatever you like,' he said, setting his empty bowl on the table. Drips of the red soup ran onto the wood and Robbie watched Wendy eyeing them.

'The doctor said you should spend as much time in bed as you can for the first few days,' Robbie said.

'I've never heard the like of all this,' his father said, attempting to stand. When Wendy tried to help him, he pushed away her hand and they watched as he made his way across the room by grabbing on to bits and pieces of furniture.

'I set you up in the other room there, Dad. So you don't need to be bothered climbing the stairs.'

John muttered something under his breath and changed direction, trying his best to slam the door behind him. As Wendy started to unpack his hospital bag, she set the Bob Dylan record on the coffee table, still intact in its sleeve. Robbie picked at the Sellotape, removed the large black disk and went in search of the record player.

'Robbie . . .' Wendy said but then stopped herself.

After almost an hour of searching, he recovered it from a pile of odds and ends in the shed and set it on the deep windowsill in the living room where it used to sit. The dust from the lid made him sneeze and Wendy squeezed past him on her way to the kitchen and wiped it clean without meeting his eye. Through the crackle the harmonica sounded and Robbie sank into a chair to listen.

Fifteen

Days on the farm felt more like a series of tests engineered to exhaust Robbie's patience. John had struck an unhappy medium between complete bed rest and full-time farming. He chose to prop himself up with an old walking stick and loiter in the doorframes of the house, barking orders at his son. More drill sergeant than father, John seemed determined that Robbie complete the tasks to as high a standard as possible.

Robbie inherited several incomplete projects that his father had ambitiously begun: a half-built chicken coop, a structure for a compost heap and a complicated pigeon decoy to lure the birds into the yard where they could be shot. His father gave him detailed instructions as to how the projects should be completed and put the pigeon decoy as top priority.

'I've drawn a diagram for this one,' his father said, grunting in recognition of the cup of tea Robbie had set in front of him.

'Which one?'

'The pigeon decoy. It's on your list.'

'What do I need a diagram for?'

'Those birds aren't stupid,' he said, setting the piece of paper down to stress his point. 'They'll be sitting up in that tree just laughing at our contraptions. It has to be convincing.'

Robbie reached for the diagram.

'What is that?' he said, pointing at the scribbles on the top of the structure his father had sketched.

'Feathers.'

'What?'

'Pigeon feathers,' he explained as if to a child. 'I told you, it has to look believable.'

'And where do you expect me to get those?'

His father lifted his arms to hold an invisible gun and, pinching one eye closed, mimed pulling the trigger.

'No way,' Robbie said.

'You were a pretty decent shot back in the day.'

'I was a child. I shot a few pheasants from close range. I don't think that qualifies.'

'Don't be modest.'

Robbie's hand twitched around his cup. He could remember the feel of the trigger beneath his finger and the heavy weight of the gun. He was only fourteen when he hit his first target, a pregnant rabbit that used to wreak havoc in their vegetable garden. Two years later his father took him to his shooting club on Saturdays where pheasants were reared to be shot.

As a youth, plucking a bird from the sky gave him a sense of accomplishment. He would stand for a moment with his gun pointing at the clouds where the bird had flown only seconds before and then lower it slowly, savouring the moment. When the dog had sniffed it out, Robbie would force himself to stand perfectly still beside the thicket until the dog emerged with the bird in its teeth and dropped it at his feet. It was amusing to remember himself, small and thin at the table of the sports club beside the other men shovelling spoonfuls of stew down their throats.

He couldn't have been more than fifteen when shots were fired in the night and he found himself standing in his pyjamas at the other end of his father's gun. It must have been during the winter months because he felt the cold cobblestones beneath his feet despite his thick bed socks. Opening the door of the shed to see his father slumped in an old armchair with a gun in his lap had felt like a dream.

The whiskey was strong on his breath and two empty bottles quivered on the shelf, despite his best efforts to shoot them down. Margaret had sent Robbie out, with that weary tone of voice that had long since given up hope of anything changing. As he padded down the stairs, pulled on a coat and unbolted the back door, he blamed himself for not hiding the gun better. His mother had given him the task of concealing it several weeks before and he had half-heartedly slid it behind the empty jam jars in the utility room cupboard. With one hand gripping the door handle, Robbie stood silently as his father raised the gun to his shoulder, the barrel bobbing in the direction of Robbie's face as though the gun were afloat.

He had lifted his hands to declare his innocence. It was a silly thing but there seemed little else to do in the moment. John started shouting and swearing, most of it incoherent, and his eyes were so red-rimmed that Robbie wasn't sure what he was seeing.

'You're not man enough to hold a gun until you can stand at the other end of one,' he had shouted, half-closing his eye to get a better aim.

The rest of the provocations blurred in Robbie's memory but the realisation that he might die was clear in his mind. He was definitely frightened but not in a sweaty, panicked kind of way; it was more like an acceptance of something that he could do nothing to change.

The shed was poorly lit by a single bare bulb, which dangled from a beam in the roof and caused shadows to lengthen on the stone walls around them. When their aging German Shepherd stirred in the corner, it took Robbie several minutes to register what it was, too late to prevent his father from spinning round with the gun and sending a bullet into the darkness. Deaf from old age, the dog had not minded the ramblings of its owner as he drank himself into a fury. It was not until it registered

Robbie's presence that the dog roused itself. Up close, the noise of the gunshot was deafening as it ricocheted off the walls and lodged itself as an echo in Robbie's head. He had been unable to move but kept staring into the corner, his heart beating faster as his eyes adjusted and he was able to piece together the howling with the bloody body of the dog. John dropped his gun on the floor, attempted to stand up and then thought better of it, sinking into the chair and closing his eyes. Looking from his father to the darkened corner where his dog lay, Robbie had started to cry. Unable to see where the animal had been shot, he knelt on the floor and cradled it while the blood made a paste on the dusty floor.

For years the memory of the dying dog haunted him. At the time it must have happened quite quickly but it played out in slow motion now any time he thought of it. It had been up to him to transport it in a wheelbarrow to the back of the orchard. It was Robbie who dug the grave by torchlight beside the apple trees. It was his responsibility to concoct a likely story of the dog's disappearance, for years suffering his sisters' wrath for allegedly leaving the cattle gate open for him to escape. He wondered did his mother know. Did she hear him scrubbing at the blood stains in the laundry room, or crying himself to sleep after half-carrying his father onto the sofa?

Now, as he watched his father add pen strokes to his sketch of the pigeon decoy, he considered the likely possibility that he too believed the dog had run away.

'Dad?'

'What?'

'Whatever happened to Tess?'

His father didn't look up from the page.

'You know what happened to her.'

Robbie stood to clear the breakfast dishes and listened while his father explained the exact dimensions of the wood he needed to buy and the tools he should use.

୫୦

The town centre was quiet, apart from the men hanging bunting for the Twelfth of July parades. On one side of the square, scaffolding was being used to to erect a large wooden arch that straddled the road; fake bricks had been painted on it to give the impression of a wall. A portrait of the Queen eyeballed passersby and Robbie stood awhile under her watchful gaze, wondering what she made year in, year out, of the uniformed flute players, orange flags, baton twirling and lambeg drumming that went on beneath her.

'Well I'll be,' said one of the men hammering together the structure. 'I'd know those ears anywhere. Robbie Hanright, how the fuck are you?'

'Adrian Green? Good to see you.'

Robbie stepped closer to shake his hand and was able to recognise the features of his high school friend in a much fatter face. He was wearing paint-spattered overalls and heavy work boots. His hair was thin and cut short and spiky.

'What are you like gaping up at this here arch? Long time no see.'

Adrian had stepped away from his workmates to light a cigarette and Robbie turned one down when offered. His last memory of Adrian was of seeing him sitting outside the school gates in a Fiesta, the car waxed to a shine with wing mirrors that the girls looked into to apply their lipstick. He had dropped out after GCSEs to work in his father's shop and was one of the first boys Robbie knew to own a car.

'I moved to Dublin a few years ago—'

'I heard that, aye.'

Robbie hesitated.

'You did?'

'Oh aye. Sure you can't keep much secret around here.'

'No, I'd say not.'

Adrian drew sharply on his cigarette.

'Sorry to hear about your da.'

'Thanks.'

'That's why you're home then, aye?'

'Yep, just a passing family visit.'

Adrian threw his half-smoked cigarette on the pavement and slapped Robbie on the back as he exhaled.

'Good man. I won't be bumping into you again then, I'd imagine.'

He looked at Robbie as though it were a question.

'Like I said, Adrian, a passing visit.'

'Right. I'll be getting back to work. Take care.'

He tugged at his overalls and gave Robbie a mock salute. As the men went in opposite directions, Robbie looked back over his shoulder to see Adrian explaining something to his workmates.

℃

With various lengths of wood poking out of the boot, Robbie arrived back at the house with a steely determination to build the pigeon decoy. The care he took in working out the measurements of the structure his father had described and the thought he put in to the choice of wood and fixtures was so consuming that he had time for little else that day. The conversation with Adrian did not come back to him until much later that afternoon. The light was starting to fade and he took one of the beers he had hidden in the shed out to the orchard. The apple trees were green with new leaves and the long summer days gave the impression that it was much earlier than it seemed. He walked to the perimeter of the house and sat on the gate that opened into the field beyond. The beer was not cold enough and Robbie felt his spirits low as the sun hovered on the horizon. Adrian's father was in the UVF. It was inevitable that Adrian would learn the ropes, settle in Dromore, drink in Boyle's, and become good at issuing subtle threats.

He remembered his form one class, seated that first day in

alphabetical order, wearing blazers several sizes too big and short, smart haircuts. The class was an odd mix of boys who had raced towards puberty and those whose mothers had held them back a while; girls who had discovered make-up and those who bought horse magazines to collect the posters.

Robbie was still very naïve but not intimidated by girls because he had grown up with sisters. That became his passport to cool, with boys like Adrian using him as their go-between while they found hideouts to smoke and swap pornographic pictures. Something in Adrian had always scared him. He would make a statement and then eyeball his listeners so that it was impossible to contradict him. He told the rudest jokes, showed no fear of teachers and seemed to spend the majority of his time in the chair outside the headmaster's office looking bored. But there was something attractive about him that Robbie could never quite walk away from. His proper friends were not impressed by Adrian's bravado and did not understand Robbie's fascination. They wanted to walk into town to buy sandwiches on their lunch break and get together at the weekends to play computer games or go fishing. Robbie enjoyed that too but whenever Adrian called, Robbie went to him, driven by curiosity and awe.

As the years passed and the boys grew into their blazers, Robbie realised he was smart and started to listen to his teachers when they told him that if he worked hard he would be able to get any job he liked. This was around the same time Adrian was befriended by older boys and he started showing less and less interest in school. When the GCSE results were handed out and Robbie caught Adrian's eyes across the hall, he felt that something was understood between them. It should not have surprised him when, six years later, Adrian Green's name cropped up in some correspondence that Martin received and it was passed on to Robbie to investigate. He did not even bother to claim a loyalty to his former school friend, such was the thirst of his journalistic youth.

How had Adrian shaken his hand and asked after his father with such a convincing look of concern? He had even offered Robbie a cigarette, as though it were a Friday afternoon in 1999 and they were waiting at the bus stop. Robbie shivered. Their meeting had unnerved him. He tried to turn his thoughts to the pigeon decoy and the work that would be completed in the morning. Once the basic structure was finished, he would have the unpleasant task of sourcing feathers to make it look believable. His stomach gurgled and he suddenly jumped down from the gate, threw his beer can into the hedge and ran towards the house.

'Where the hell have you been?' his father hollered from the living room.

'Sorry, I lost track of time.' Robbie washed his hands in the kitchen sink.

'I'm hungry.'

'Yes, I know. I said I was sorry.'

'I thought your being here meant I wouldn't go hungry and nor would the animals. By the sound of that cow, I'd say her dinner's been forgotten an'all.'

'Shit.'

'That's what I thought.'

Robbie heard in his father's voice a delight at being proved right and suddenly he wanted to take a hammer to the decoy under construction in the shed. The volume went up on the television and Robbie pulled the kitchen door over to put some distance between them. After feeding the animals, Robbie searched the cupboards for food. It had been a long time since he had cooked. Hannah normally disappeared into the kitchen while he was filing his stories and emerge later with curry or soup. The tins and cartons Wendy had delivered the previous day did not inspire any ideas for a meal and he began to panic.

'Wendy, it's me. No, no, nothing's wrong. Well, yes I suppose something is wrong but it's not serious. I was just wondering if you could help me out, I'm in a bit of a pickle. Are you busy? Sorry, yes, I'll spit it out. It's just . . . I don't know how to cook.'

There was silence on the other end of the phone, then a deep sigh.

'I really am sorry to— Really? I wasn't expecting that, I just thought maybe. . . Well I don't know what I was expecting exactly, I just needed help. Right, very well then, I'll see you soon.'

He put down the phone and ran his hands through his hair, wishing there was something stronger in the house than the orange juice Wendy had left in the fridge.

Sixteen

'His colour seems to have improved,' Wendy said, handing Robbie a can of tomatoes and a tin opener.

'He's being sick a lot,' he said.

'That's the painkillers.'

'I know, it's just not nice to listen to.'

'Well,' she said, turning to him. 'You can rest assured that it's worse for him.'

'I didn't mean it like that. I don't like hearing him in pain, that's all.'

Wendy poured the tomatoes into the pan and stirred slowly. 'How do you think he'll cope tomorrow?'

Robbie found a bag of crisps in the cupboard and set them on the counter between them.

'I don't know. I'm assuming it won't be as traumatic as the operation. He won't feel a thing and it will all be over quite quickly; at least that's what the oncologist said.'

'I don't remember even having a conversation about it.'

'It was the day of the op; we were all pretty tired.'

Wendy put the lid on the pot and stuck her head into the living room to make sure that her children were behaving.

'Telly addicts,' she said and pulled up a chair at the kitchen table. 'Sorry I can't be there tomorrow.'

'Don't worry, not everyone can swan about the country like me.'

The noise from the television was muffled by the closed door but what sounded like explosions and men screaming were still audible.

'So what exactly do you write about in that column of yours?' Wendy asked, her tone more gentle than Robbie was used to.

'Cultural stuff. You know, five hundred words on how Eastern European music is becoming popular in dingy Dublin bars or how the sculptures erected in Merrion Square give the Georgian garden a hideous modern edge.'

'People want to read your opinion on those things?'

'Apparently so.'

'Do you enjoy it?' She did not look at him but busied herself searching for something in her handbag. Robbie considered the question.

'Sometimes I do and sometimes it's just a job. I often wonder whether anything I write is really what I think. People love the column because I just speak my mind, often quite harshly, but the truth is my opinions are just as shaped by what my readers want to hear as any other columnist. Maybe I don't think the director's choice to cast so-and-so in the latest film is unimaginative but I know that's what will upset my readers, so that's what I write. It's all very messed up.'

'Well. I wonder what they'd think about you if they knew you couldn't cook to save your life.' She stood up to check the bubbling pot and took potatoes out of the cupboard beside the sink. With three large ones in her hand, she looked at Robbie with a furrowed brow.

'Dad doesn't eat very much; he lost his appetite completely when he started getting sick. When he does eat, it's simple: potatoes, a piece of meat and some veg. He's not going to like this.' She pointed at the stove. 'But if I fried him that piece of meat, it'd be as tough as an old boot. He likes beef the best but too much red meat is bad, so my general rule is chicken, fish or pork twice a week. A pork chop always goes down well. Make sure it's cooked through though; that's important.'

She was striking the potato with the peeler as if it might produce a spark.

'Never cook fish on a Friday; he'll refuse to eat it. And don't give him anything but the breast of the chicken; he turns his nose up at the dark meat.'

Robbie took the potatoes and the peeler from her as if she were a child handling a dangerous object. He wasn't sure if he was meant to respond to her ramblings and something in her tone was unstable and rather frightening.

'*You* have to put the salt on his food. If you give him the salt shaker, he'll use far too much. And he takes a glass of milk with his meal and a cup of tea afterwards. The grill is handy enough to use. You just pull this out and put a baking tray on the shelf, not too near the top or the meat will burn before it's cooked.'

She moved quickly around the kitchen, opening drawers and alerting Robbie to their contents. He had paused in his peeling to watch her furious energy being expended on household items and he began to feel afraid.

'There's a stack of meat in here,' she said, opening the freezer. 'Enough to do you this week at least. Oh, for lunch he likes a slice of corned beef in a roll. Well, he doesn't like rolls, prefers two bits of bread, but I always buy rolls.' She laughed, but it was too out of place to join in. 'One slice of beef, no, two slices and one slice of tomato, or is it two slices of tomato?'

Her voice was increasing in volume and pitch as she pulled bits of food out of the fridge: a tin of corned beef, a bag of tomatoes, cheese. Things were falling on the ground as she rummaged and a cartoon of cream burst on the linoleum and covered her shoes. He watched as her arms flailed like the blades of a helicopter, and knew he should go to her but instead took a step back and pressed himself against the oven.

Her hair had broken free from its ponytail and gave her the

look of a madwoman who had lost something so precious that there was neither room nor time for decorum. She gripped the kitchen counter with both hands and made a sound like a dog barking. Her entire body heaved as though she was a drunken teenager vomiting in a ditch. It was not until the door opened that Robbie could shake himself into action.

'Mum?' came his nephew's voice from behind the door. Robbie moved quickly past Wendy to shoo the boy out of the room.

'Your mum is making Granddad a lovely dinner and you, little rascal, are meant to be keeping the old boy entertained.'

'What's going on in there?' John asked, looking at the closed kitchen door.

He looked shrivelled in the large sofa and Robbie noticed that his colour had definitely not improved.

'You know Wendy – ever the perfectionist when it comes to grub,' Robbie said.

'Well, go on then, give her a hand and get things going.' He turned back to the television on which men dressed in camouflage were covered in muck and blood.

'Are you sure the boys should be watching that?' Robbie asked. The two of them were open-mouthed and staring at the screen.

'Augh sure, they're old enough to know about war.'

Back in the kitchen Wendy had composed herself and was drinking a glass of water.

'We're ready to go here,' she said, opening the cutlery drawer noisily.

'Wendy—'

'What?' She turned to face him, spatula in hand and eyes so fierce that Robbie had to look away.

'Nothing.'

She started dishing out the thick stew into two bowls.

'You're not eating?'

'It's eight o'clock at night, Robbie. We had our tea hours ago and so should he have.'

'Of course.'

Her tone was condescending again and Robbie relaxed.

John scoffed at the food as Wendy had predicted and she rolled her eyes behind his back as she gathered her children's things. After she left, Robbie and his father sat in silence as men fell prey to mortar attacks on the screen. His sister's outburst had shaken him so badly that he was unable to finish his food and both men's bowls sat half-eaten in their laps. As the credits appeared, Robbie could hear his father snoring and sat still beside him to allow him to sleep. He tried to imagine all the nights John had spent sitting on the sofa alone. Did he find peace in the silence when the tractors were in for the night and the lane was quiet, or did he wish for company in front of the lit fire?

Memories of his father in the armchair, hidden away behind a newspaper, came back to him. It was his way of shutting out the rest of them, abandoning his family without leaving the room. Robbie could remember his mother appealing to the front cover of the broadsheet when he and his sisters were misbehaving but his father would re-cross his legs and ignore them all.

Now he had his isolation, Robbie wondered whether it was how he wanted to live out the rest of his days. There had never been talk of another woman, as far as he knew, and Robbie found it impossible to imagine the type of wife his father would need to be happy. His mother was too flighty and unstable. Robbie could see that, even as a child. With three children and a farmhouse of animals, she fought so hard to work out who she was.

As a mother, she was particular, but removed. At her best there was food on the table at 5pm; at her worst she cobbled something together out of the empty cupboards: tinned ham, rice and carrots or a combination of raw vegetables in the shape of a smiley face on their plates. Looking back now, Robbie wondered how she had lasted so long. She was a housewife and mother at the age of twenty-two with an alcoholic husband and very little money generated from their farm.

He tried to remember her then, as a woman and not just as his mother. She would have been standing in the living room wedged into a corner by the ironing board with the three of them running between the rooms creating a draft; or elbow deep in hand-washing in the kitchen while Robbie demanded to be told where his rugby kit was; or dunking the girls in the bath, sometimes washing their hair, sometimes forgetting for days; or collapsed at the end of the night in a corner of the sofa with a cup of tea and some sewing, quiet and contemplating things that Robbie suddenly wanted to understand.

He thought of her now and the disorder of her brightly lit kitchen and he smiled. She had given so much of the early part of her life to her ungrateful husband and children and was now reclaiming the last part in high-heeled shoes and patterned scarves.

'What are you smirking about?' his father asked.

'I thought you were asleep.'

'I was not indeed.'

'I was thinking about Mum.'

His father made no acknowledgement.

'It's just strange being back and her not being here, that's all.'

'You'll get used to it,' he mumbled.

'Like you have?'

Robbie watched as his father spat a piece of meat back into his bowl.

'I can't eat another mouthful of this,' he said, struggling to push himself off the sofa. Robbie got up to help him.

'Get away from me. I'm fine as I am.'

'Very well, do it yourself,' he said, and piled the dishes on the tray to take into the kitchen. When he went back into the living room, his father was standing beside the sofa, breathing heavily.

'I'm going to bed,' he said between gasps. 'I'll be washed and dressed by nine.'

ᘒ

'And who are you?' Robbie's father asked the young woman who tried to guide him by the arm.

'I am the radiographer, Mr. Hanright. I'll be helping with your consultation this morning.'

Her hair was blonde and smelt of coconut, Robbie smiled at her as though his father was a shared joke between them.

'Who was that Chinky then? I thought she was the radio . . . radiog . . . radia—'

'Radiologist, Dad. Dr Chan is your radiologist and this young woman,' he looked closer at her badge, 'Patrice, is a radiographer. They do different things.'

His father, satisfied by his explanation, shook Patrice's hand from his arm and made for the cubicle to change. He closed the door on her while she was in the middle of giving him instructions. Robbie shrugged and apologised.

Dr. Chan spoke to them both kindly. She was a small woman in a large white coat with shiny, short black hair and a tiny nose. Her gesticulations were feline as she described the process that lay ahead of Robbie's father. The simulator, she explained, was like a spaceship but that shouldn't put him off. It wouldn't cause any pain and was used to determine the best area to focus the radiotherapy in order to kill the most cancer cells. Robbie had nodded professionally as though he were interviewing her and the process she was describing was for someone unknown to him.

Patrice allowed him to have a look at the room. He found the machine intimidating. The plastic looked squeaky clean and

114

nurses were dressing the bed beneath it in a thin white covering. Trying to imagine the withered body of his father lying beneath the huge eye of the simulator was disturbing.

'Will he be radioactive when he's finished?' he asked the nurses. They shared knowing glances before one of them replied.

'No, love,' she said, placing a hand on his arm.

The door of the changing room opened and Robbie slipped out before his father suffered the embarrassment of being seen in the hospital gown.

In the hallway, Robbie remembered how he had paced the corridors of the National Maternity Hospital when Hannah was in labour. The recycled air of the ward suffocated him and he would walk into Merrion Square where the statue of Oscar Wilde kept him company.

He remembered the dripping leaves and how the art sellers had to shelter under tarpaulins on the Sunday his daughter was born. One of the paintings would forever be linked to the beginning of his life as a father. It was of a little girl in a red raincoat standing on a beach. The oil paint made thick blobs of cloud above her and the wind picked up the edges of her clothes. She was all alone in a great expanse of sand, sea and sky, standing firm against the gale, looking out to sea as though she had lost something. He stood for so long in front of the painting that the artist approached him twice, just to make sure he was not interested in buying it. It was her isolation that stunned him. She was small and unprotected and it made him feel guilty.

He had not realised, until then, how strong the pull was to run away. Hannah's growing stomach had looked as though it would burst and pour all sorts of things on his future he was not ready for. The miracle of pregnancy had been lost on him. It was foreign and existed outside of him, so much so that he started to wonder if he was needed at all. But the small, stoic figure of a girl alone on a beach stirred something paternal in him and convinced him to stay.

Seventeen

Margaret had made brown onion soup for lunch and Wendy, Robbie and Elizabeth arrived at the house within minutes of one another.

'Are we waiting for Adam?' Robbie asked as his mother cut the bread.

'No, it's just the four of us. Grab some butter from the fridge, will you, Elizabeth?'

Wendy washed her hands in the sink before sitting down. Her nervousness seemed to spread as Elizabeth fidgeted at the table and a quiet settled in the room.

'I may as well just get on with it—'

'Excuse me, son. We'll say grace first, thank you very much.'

No one spoke as their mother ladled soup into the bowls in front of them. Robbie bent forward to smell it and closed his eyes. He drifted back to the farmhouse and remembered the days starting to lengthen and the expectation of summer in the air while the last of the onions bulged in the vegetable patch.

'For what we are about to receive may the Lord make us truly thankful.'

'Amen,' they echoed.

There was no other sound apart from the clink of their spoons against the crockery.

'Go on then,' Wendy said.

The soup scorched the inside of his mouth and he took a drink of water.

'As you know, the surgery didn't go as well as we'd hoped; there were still some cancer cells that they weren't able to remove. I spoke quite extensively to Dr. Chan – sorry, the radiologist. She explained that there's a team appointed to work out a treatment plan for Dad's radiotherapy and that the procedure today was only to pinpoint the area where he needs the therapy to be focused.' He exhaled loudly. 'Basically he has to go in every day this week for treatment.'

'And will the cells be gone after that?' Elizabeth asked.

Despite the fact that the sun had been shining all morning, Robbie shivered and leant over his bowl of soup so that the steam might warm his face.

'The treatment is more about slowing the growth, not taking it away altogether. They don't often use it as a treatment because it can damage healthy cells, but they think that in Dad's case it's worth giving him a week and then see how he's doing.'

Wendy sat back in her seat and he wondered if she was going to cry. 'I don't know if I can take much more of this,' she said, looking at her mother. 'More waiting and "what ifs" – surely there's more they can do?'

Her spoon hovered over the bowl and no one met her eye.

'I suppose we just have to hope that he's in the twenty-four percent,' Elizabeth said.

'What?' Wendy set her spoon down.

'Don't you remember that the doctor said twenty-four percent survival rate?'

Robbie met Wendy's eye across the table.

'Lizzie darling,' Robbie started, 'what the doctor said was that twenty-four per cent survive for a year after the kind of surgery that Dad had.'

He heard his mother's sharp intake of breath and realised that the statistic was news to her. With head bent over her lunch, she buttered a slice of bread until it fell apart.

When Robbie's grandmother died, he remembered finding

his mother on the floor of the utility room wearing rubber gloves and scrubbing the linoleum. All anguish and loss was diluted in that bucket of bleach, poured out on the pale yellow floor and worked into such a lathered frenzy that some of the pattern was worn away. With steely determination she focused on the task of preparing the funeral. The sandwiches were perfectly triangular, the teapot was never empty and guests were encouraged to talk until they ran out of things to say. But she rarely spoke, never sat down and did not shed a tear that Robbie had seen. Although she encouraged the children to go in and look at the body, she always found a reason to keep away: the kettle needed boiling, the potatoes wouldn't peel themselves, or she heard the phone ringing when it never was. Robbie was fifteen, old enough to know that there was something quite unnatural about her behaviour but too young to know what to say or how to help.

'Are you sure?' Elizabeth asked.

'He's right,' Wendy said, taking her spoon up again. 'We need to prepare ourselves for the worst.'

Elizabeth gasped.

'Wendy—'

'There's no point nurturing any false hope. He's going to die from this. It's just a question of how soon and what we can do to prolong his life.'

'Why?'

It was the first time their mother had spoken. Robbie was surprised by how set her jaw was and how calmly she brought the soup spoon to her lips. He felt his stomach turn over.

'What do you mean, "why"?' Wendy asked and Elizabeth agreed.

Their mother sighed and looked from one of them to the other.

'Hasn't he taken enough of your time and energy? Aren't you tired? Why is it so important to prolong what is more accurately his death and not his life? You're going to spend months trying to care for him, suffering his bitterness and spite, because, trust me, he's not going to go quietly – and for what? The outcome won't change. I just . . . I just don't want to see you all go through that.'

The room was so still when she had finished that Robbie could hear a car starting on the main road. He struggled to interpret his sisters' silence. His eyes flickered between them, trying to gauge their reaction but their faces were blank.

'What do you suggest we do, Mother?' Wendy said, her lips tight and eyebrows raised. 'Give up? Walk away? Abandon him? Oh yes, I forgot, that's exactly what you'd have us do. That way we'd be following in your footsteps and you wouldn't have to feel guilty about your choices. Well it doesn't work like that for us. We're all he's got left, his next of kin, his blood relatives. Whether you think he deserves it or not, we can't just leave him to waste away.'

Pushing her soup violently into the middle of the table, she stood up and started to gather her things. Her whole body was shaking from the confrontation.

'Wendy, please, don't go, we can talk—'

'Talk about what, Mother? About ways to speed up his death so we can all get on with our lives? Or, or, what we might do with his assets when he's gone – is that what you thought this conversation was about? Perhaps you'd prefer to talk about the fact that, thanks to you, looking after him takes up so much of my time that I haven't had the energy to sleep with my husband for God knows how long and he's off with some tart from the office. Which of those scintillating conversations would you like to have?'

'Oh Wendy,' Elizabeth said quietly.

'No, Elizabeth, don't you dare feel sorry for me,' she said, wiping tears away so roughly that her cheeks started to glow red. 'Don't you dare!'

The fight was draining out of her and she took hold of the

rest of her belongings wearily. Robbie held her car keys, his mind racing to think of some way to resolve the conversation. So much had been said and both Wendy and his mother looked emptied out and tired.

'I'll walk you out,' he said.

Outside the sky had clouded over and the grey afternoon was hanging oppressively above them. Robbie loitered beside the car while Wendy packed her belongings in the boot and got into the driver's seat.

'We should divide up the runs to the hospital,' she said, putting her key in the ignition.

'Nah, don't worry about that. Sure, what else will I be doing?' Robbie said.

Wendy sighed and stared vacantly at the garden behind him.

'I never thought I'd say this, Robbie, but I'm glad you came back.'

She pulled the car door shut before he had a chance to respond. The wheels spun on the gravel and he lifted his hand to wave as she revved the car out of the driveway. The wind was cold and for a brief moment Robbie thought he might cry. After taking several deep breaths and paying close inspection to a bed of tulips nodding in the breeze, he regained control.

He thought of his house in Dublin, his daughter spread-eagled on the living room carpet, surrounded by brightly coloured building bricks. He could smell the new paint on the living room walls – light grey, designed to bring light into the room. The details of his life, about which he had once been ambivalent, he now gathered around him like a blanket against the cold. He could see the colour card that Hannah had left lying on the living room table for weeks in the hope that he would be interested enough to look at it. Standing in the front driveway of his mother's house, he wished he could go back there and have a discussion with his wife about the subtle difference between Nordic Spa and Pacific Breeze.

'Robbie?' Elizabeth called from the doorway. 'Your soup is getting cold.'

Back in the kitchen the conversation had turned to Adam. His mother was telling Elizabeth about a contract he had been given to service a fleet of taxis.

'It's the kind of thing that will no doubt lead to more business. You know? He's working so hard but it will be worth it. It really will.'

As she spoke, she touched her hair and fiddled with her rings. Her voice had a high-pitched quality to it that betrayed how much Wendy had ruffled her feathers. Being around women so much was beginning to wear Robbie down.

'Sounds great, Mum,' Elizabeth said through a yawn, eyeing Robbie as he paced the kitchen.

'Mum—'

'Robbie, Mum was just talking about Adam,' Elizabeth said, grabbing him as he walked past the back of her chair.

'Yes, so I heard but I don't quite think we can move on without clearing up our earlier conversation. Don't you agree?' He looked at the two women and felt awed at the way they bent to him, pulling up chairs at the table obediently.

Hannah came to mind and that slightly sick feeling of knowing that things were not right between them rose in his throat. It was a truth he had taken great pains to avoid. Now that his emotional compass was being assaulted on every side, he no longer had the facilities to pick and choose his reactions to things. In the middle of his mother's kitchen, with the remains of onion soup clotting on the tablecloth, he realised that if he did not do something to fix his marriage, he could end up just like his father. With his mother's face so etched with wrinkles and sun damage in front of him, he tried to picture Hannah and his daughter sitting at a kitchen table in years to come, trying to fob him off onto one another, wishing him dead.

'Son, are you ok? Your face has gone white and you're awful quiet.'

He cleared his throat.

'Sorry, I was just thinking about Hannah.'

His mother smiled in Elizabeth's direction.

'Of course you're missing her. It's a brave lot of time to be spending away from your wife and child. We'll sort all this mess out and you'll be back in no time.'

Robbie nodded.

'About to our earlier conversation,' he began, drawing back his shoulders. 'Mum, I'm sorry to say that you're his next of kin which makes you the main decision-maker in this whole thing. We can be here to discuss it with you, of course, but you're still his wife.'

He had avoided her eye while he spoke and focused on running a tea towel through his hands. As silence fell around the table, he and Elizabeth both watched for a reaction.

'That is absolutely ridiculous,' she said, her saliva like accompanying punctuation. 'I haven't had an opinion on your father's life for years. How can it possibly be down to me? We've not spoken a cordial word to one another since the day I closed the door on that farmhouse. Can't the three of you sort this out? I only had you all here today so that I could support my children, not so that I could get involved. I can't be expected to make a decision about his best interests. I'm far too bitter to be trusted with anything of the sort.'

'There's no use petitioning me, Mother. I'm not the one making you do it; it's the law. You're legally his wife and his next of kin. It's really that simple,' countered Robbie.

Elizabeth, who had been sitting quietly until then, reached out to take her mother's hand.

'It doesn't mean anything, Mum. We all know the history here and we're in it together, as a family.'

'My family is you children, not him. He stopped being my family a long time ago, d'you hear me, Robbie? I may be his wife on paper but that never stopped him treating me like I was nothing and it won't stop me from refusing to acknowledge him as husband, next of kin or whatever else you want to call him. I won't do it and that's the end of it.'

Her chair scraped loudly on the kitchen floor as she stood up and left the room. Robbie exhaled and fell back in his chair.

'Two females storming out of a room in the space of an hour, now that's quite something, even for me,' he said.

Elizabeth laughed and put her forehead on the tablecloth.

'Drink?'

'Only if you promise not to storm out on me this time,' he said.

'Promise.'

'Right you are then, grab your coat.'

Eighteen

The week of radiotherapy passed quickly. The routine of early mornings, driving up and down the A3 and afternoons listening to his father snoring in bed settled Robbie. He assumed the role of organiser and acquired a way of speaking to his father that attempted to make light of his situation. The planning and detail of his day blocked the reality of his father's illness and by the evening Robbie collapsed into bed without so much as a thought about anything serious.

ഇ

When Wendy called over in the afternoons, he went outside and left her sitting at their father's side. Robbie had taken on the flowerbeds in front of the house as a project. The local nursery had a buy-one-get-one-free deal on and he chose various bedding plants that would brighten up the driveway and improve the view out of his father's bedroom window.

As he worked, he wondered what his father made of him. The most he had ever heard him say was the night he packed up to leave for Dublin. So many of the details of that evening were hazy but his father's body in the doorframe of Robbie's room, and the way he gripped his shoulders before pressing an envelope full of £20 notes into his hand were impossible to forget.

For some reason that Robbie could not remember, he had not turned the lights on in his bedroom while he packed. He had taken the biggest suitcase in the attic and put all the clothes and books he could fit into it. His father could have been standing there for several minutes but when Robbie saw him silhouetted against the hall light, he had jumped and sworn loudly.

'Sometimes it takes a braver man to run away, son,' his father had said. The tone of his voice had stopped Robbie dead. There was a quality to his words that he had never heard before: measured, firm and yet kind. The affirmation it communicated took Robbie down the stairs, into the car and across the border. It gave him the impetus to stay away and he used it, rightly or wrongly, to justify his not returning home for five years.

A car was driving slowly down the road and Robbie heard it stop behind him. Moving towards the gate, he used his hand to shield his eyes from the sun and recognised the woman driving as Martin's wife, Joan. They stared at one another for several seconds before she rolled down the window.

'Fancy a drive?'

After taking off his gardening gloves and glancing at his reflection in the hall window, Robbie got into the car.

She drove in the direction of Murphy's Lane and he laughed.

'What?' she said.

'Seems like no time has passed at all.'

'It's not like that,' she said, her cheeks flushed.

Out of the corner of his eye Robbie could see that she was wearing make-up and the effect pleased him. There was almost something maternal in the way she had courted him as a young journalist. After feeding him alongside her children, she would put the little ones to bed and sit for hours with him in the living room watching television and asking about his family. He talked to her in a way he had never opened up to anyone and it was not long before he believed they were in love.

'You look nice,' he said.

Joan narrowed her eyes and turned away before Robbie could

be sure that he had seen her smile.

Halfway down the lane there was an old building that had deteriorated so badly that ivy had all but obliterated any sign of a dwelling. Joan pulled the car into what once would have been a driveway, turned off the engine and lit a cigarette.

He could remember lying next to her in the spare bedroom, she lighting a cigarette while he giggled and stroked her stomach. The lights were always off but he would trace the contours of her full figure by the glow of the streetlight and listen while she confessed to her unhappiness with Martin.

'My dad's got cancer,' he blurted out.

'Jesus,' she said, turning to face him.

'Sorry,' he said. 'I didn't mean to . . .'

'Don't be daft.'

'He's going downhill so fast.'

'Where is it?'

'Pancreas,' he said, taking one of her cigarettes.

'That's a bad one.'

'Yep.'

When she leant over to give him the flame from her lighter, he caught a glimpse of her cleavage.

'There was more to your da than met the eye, you know?' she said, catching his gaze and pulling up her top.

'There was?'

'All that stuff you used to tell me, you'd think he spent all his time drinking and fighting. I was in Thyme Square one day meeting my Aunt and your dad came in to fetch the kitchen scraps for his pig. That was a good while ago now, mind. Anyway, Auntie Helen blushed like a schoolgirl when he said hello to her; said he was quite the man about town in her day.'

'He was, was he?'

'She told me that he worked in the butchers on the High Street. One of your da's jobs was to deliver the orders round the town on his bicycle. He had a big, old basket on the front that he packed with all the meat that had been carved up that morning. Helen used to see him cycling up those hills like fury to get his rounds done by lunchtime when he was expected to serve customers in the shop front.

'One day, she said, he was late back and Sammy was furious. My cousin was sent out to find him and it turned out he had crashed head on into another cyclist, a young woman on her way to work. Your mother was employed then in May Daly's sewing shop with Aunt Helen and she was forever running late. Apparently she had taken a back street that brought her out halfway down the Motte and Bailey. Your father was flying down the hill at top speed, his basket still full of meat, when he collided into your mother, sending her, the meat and himself flying on to the middle of the road.

'She got off with a few scratches, but he was worse for wear, with a broken collar bone and a face that had half the road embedded in it. He lost his job on account of it and had to pay Sammy back for the meat but it marked the beginning of a courtship with your mother that became the envy of the town.'

'I never knew.'

Robbie found himself smiling at the image of his father and mother in such a hurry to get on with their separate lives and then crashing into one another with the kind of force that would accompany them throughout their marriage.

Joan pushed the butt of her cigarette out of the crack in the car window.

'Thank you,' Robbie said, 'but I'm sure you didn't bring me here to reminisce about my father.'

'I don't know why I brought you here,' she said.

'It's nice to see you.'

Robbie was unable to meet her eye. The way she drummed her fingers on the windowsill made him nervous.

'The night Martin was shot, we had waffles and sausages for tea. I remember that because he pointed a bit of sausage on his fork in my direction and said he knew my dirty little secret.'

Joan took another cigarette out of the box but did not light it.

'We were in a rush, though, and the taxi was waiting outside. It was my sister's birthday and her and Davy were waiting for us in the pub. He did it like that on purpose. It was fun for him to watch me sweat all night. God,' she said, laughing. 'I could barely take a sip of my drink, my stomach was turning over that much.'

'Joan—'

'He was mean like that. You remember that, don't you?'

'Why are you telling me all this?' Robbie said.

'Why?' she said. 'Aren't you curious?'

Her forehead was creased.

'No, not really.'

Joan stared at him.

'I thought we could talk about it.'

Robbie got out of the car. It was cold in the shade and he wished he had thought to bring a coat. He heard the driver's door slam and turned to face Joan.

'I can't do this right now, Joan. What with the cancer and my family, they're . . . they're falling apart and I'm meant to be in Dublin with my wife and child. I've just got too much going on.'

Joan put her hands on the bonnet and leaned across to him. 'Were you even going to visit me? Did it even cross your mind?'

Robbie sighed.

'I don't know.'

Joan stood up straight and shoved her hands deep into her pockets.

'Did I imagine it all, Robbie? Was there not something between us? I don't understand.' She sighed like a woman well accustomed to being disappointed and Robbie could not bear to look her in the eye.

'You are a bastard,' she said.

She made as if to walk away, then paused with her back to him.

'I know life moves on and it's not good to drag up the past but there are things I need to talk about and you're the only one I can have the conversation with. You know where I live.'

'Don't do that to me. It's not fair.'

'Fair? You're talking to me about fair? Is it fair that I lost my husband and my lover at the age of thirty-two with two small children to look after? Is it fair that my girls never knew their father? What's fair?'

'I know all that and I'm sorry, I really am. I can't help you right now, Joan, not when things are so up in the air for me.'

'When then? When you run back across the border again to your cushy life? When will you be able to help me?'

'Can't you just let it go? It's not good for you to hold on to all that.'

She scoffed. Robbie looked down at his feet and crossed his arms to ward off the wind.

'Obviously I'm wasting my time,' she said. She climbed into the car, reaching over to lock the passenger door in case Robbie had any inclination that she might drive him home. He watched the car spinning in the mud and did not step out of the way in time to avoid it splattering his jeans.

He was left alone beside the shell of a house at dusk. The light at that time of day always unnerved Robbie. It neither committed to nightfall, nor gave licence to the sun to shine. The trees writhed around him and a car backfiring in the distance made him jump and clutch his heart. Avoiding the puddles, he started to jog up the lane.

The dull ache of regret settled in the pit of his stomach and he could feel the tension at the base of his neck growing steadily into a migraine. It had been years since he had suffered from a migraine, so long in fact that he no longer carried the medication with him. Where Murphy's Lane met the Quilly Road there was a mirror to enable drivers to negotiate the bad corner. Robbie stopped as he caught a glimpse of himself, distended in the bent glass. He crossed the road for a closer look – tall, red-faced and struggling to regulate his breathing. He was pathetic. From the corner where he stood, Robbie could see the farmhouse. Wendy was drawing the curtains of his father's room and the wind was carrying a thin wisp of smoke from the chimney.

Nineteen

On the last day of his father's radiotherapy treatment, they arrived late to the hospital. It had been one of those mornings when everything had gone wrong. Robbie had woken up stiff after a poor night's sleep, only to hear the wind throwing gusts of rain against the windowpane. He had curled his body into a tight ball beneath the duvet and fallen back to sleep. Half an hour later he woke up to his father screaming up the stairs that if he didn't get out of bed immediately . . .

Neither had time for breakfast before getting into the car and finding that the petrol light was on. The stop at Sainsbury's petrol station set them back ten minutes and Robbie had to break the speed limit to make up the time.

'This'll give them even more reason to mistreat me,' his father said.

'They don't mistreat you, Dad.'

'Like hell they don't. You don't see all the poking and prodding that goes on behind closed doors. It's not professional.'

The rain, which fell in thick sheets across the road, prevented them from driving too quickly on the motorway. Everyone had their lights on and the sky was as dark as mud. At the hospital the rain was falling even heavier. It bounced off the ground as Robbie coerced his father into a wheelchair and covered him as best he could with his coat.

'You didn't think to bring a brolly?' his father shouted over the rain as they crossed the car park.

Huddles of patients stood around the hospital entrance with cigarettes held at arm's length. Some had pushed their drips all the way from the wards, and were clutching their dressing gowns against the cold. Robbie's father coughed as they negotiated the smoky cloud and Robbie smiled apologetically.

The smell still gave him cravings. He could recall a time when his first action in the morning was to roll over and light a cigarette. It tasted like eating a mouthful of soil, but his body would be craving the nicotine and it allowed him a few moments, headspace before the day took hold of him and threw him towards evening.

Inside the hospital, steam rose off Robbie's wet clothes as he negotiated the hallways to the radiology department. He had not stopped to allow his father out of the wheelchair at the entrance and he was threatening to jump if Robbie did not let him walk.

'It's just faster this way,' he told his father as he stopped around the corner from the nurses' station.

'I won't be needing your assistance any more. Go on and get yourself some coffee or whatever else it is you do to kill time. I'll meet you back here in twenty minutes.'

Every day Elizabeth went by bus to Belfast and met Robbie in the cafeteria for the time it took their father to have his treatment. She refused to travel with them and Robbie did not try to convince her. The first morning Robbie had wandered into the room and been oblivious to her. He had negotiated the coffee machine, paid for the drink and a muffin and sat down at a table before he saw her hunched over a hot chocolate and shivering. It had been raining and she had walked from the bus station without an umbrella. She did not appear to be waiting for him and seemed just as surprised to see him but went on to say that she had planned to meet him there, just to keep him company.

That morning she was consumed by the task of using the sugar from the sachets on the table to make a smiley face on her paper plate. Brown sugar created the hair and a moustache, and white sugar the eyes, nose and mouth. When Robbie sat down, she jumped and pushed the plate to the side, causing the granules to scatter across the table.

She looked just like their mother in her younger days, when large spectacles and gingham were all the rage. Pictures of his parents when they were courting were few, but his mother had kept a small album of them in the living room cabinet. The photographs were sepia and showed versions of his parents he would quite liked to have known. One in particular showed them sharing an ice cream on a stone promenade in Millisle. The wind from the sea pushed back their hair to show their pure, young faces laughing at the white blobs on their noses.

'How was the bus ride today?' he asked.

'Fine.'

They sat in silence while Robbie hacked at his muffin with a plastic knife until it had almost entirely disintegrated on the plate. He resigned himself to eating it with his fingers.

'It's pretty depressing in here, isn't it?'

'You know you don't have to come, Lizzie.'

'But I do. I don't know what else to do. I know it's daft. Yesterday I decided not to come but about twenty minutes before the bus was due to leave, I was so fidgety that the thought of being in the house was unbearable. I can't go into work either; I employed someone two months ago to run the gallery, so I could spend more time painting. Big mistake. If I was at work, at least I would be distracted.'

'It's fine,' he said, reaching for her hand. 'I'm glad you're here.'

These twenty minutes with his sister soon became the highlight of Robbie's day. He would rush to the canteen where she would be waiting with coffee for both of them and a muffin cut cleanly in two. Whether it was the neutral territory or the awareness of how short their time together was, they covered topics that had never been discussed, broached even, with the background noise of the canteen putting them both at ease.

'It was all over the news,' Elizabeth said. 'Poor Joan, having to watch that happen.'

'I know,' he said, leaning in closer. 'Do you want to know the worst of it?'

'I may as well.'

'We were having an affair.'

It was as though he had started and now he needed to squeeze all his confessions into the short sessions they had together. It was day four and so far they had covered her poor luck with men, his guilt at not treating Hannah better, their mother's relationship with Adam, and how much Elizabeth wanted to have children.

'I'm not really that shocked,' she said.

'Oh.'

'You spent so much time there, it's not a bit of wonder.'

'I know. Martin invited me for dinner one night and by the end of that month I was there most nights of the week. We were always following a story, out and about meeting people, or just sitting in pubs waiting for things to happen. They were my glory days; I felt so important and I really believed in what I was doing. Anyway, something big came up that Martin didn't want me involved in. Most stuff we covered together but this time he didn't want me to touch it. He said it was too dangerous and I was more use to him at home.

'By that time I was in there with the family. I had a place at the dinner table beside his little ones and I went over even if Martin wasn't there. Perhaps affair is romanticising it a bit. Some nights I'd sit with Joan until midnight watching telly and then she'd say I could just crash in the spare room. In the morning I'd go to work with Martin like we were family. But over those few weeks it was rare that he'd be home before the wee hours of the morning and Joan and I got more and more comfortable.'

'Did he ever find out?'

Robbie hung his head.

'The night he was murdered, before he and Joan went to the pub, she phoned me to say that he knew. She didn't know how he knew but she told me to stay away for a while. I should've known he'd find out – he was a damn good investigative journalist, for God's sake. That's why I wasn't in the pub that night. For all I know, they could have shot me too. Everyone knew Martin and I were partners.'

'Oh Robbie,' she sighed. 'How do you live with something like that?'

He laughed.

'It's not that bad.'

'That's what worries me.'

'What do you mean?'

'That you don't think it's that bad.'

Robbie checked his watch.

'I'd better go. Dad will be finished.'

'Me too.'

They embraced.

As he walked away, he stole a glance over his shoulder before he left the room. Elizabeth had sat down again and looked so young and tired, it stopped him in his tracks. From the doorway he watched her holding her head in her hands, her grief so private and contained. He wanted to return to the table and say something to make her laugh, but nothing came to mind and the thought of his father's wrath took him up the corridor and into the lift.

Twenty

After a week of treatment, Robbie's father was gaunt and tired. Sitting in the oncology waiting room, he looked like a man who had just emerged from a concentration camp. Too tired to sit up straight, he was slumped in the wheelchair and trying hard to fight sleep. His skin was pale and loose and his fingers looked skeletal in the sleeves of his coat.

'With all the radiotherapy and the travelling, your father is bound to be tired,' the consultant explained when they had been ushered into his office.

'I'm not dead yet,' Robbie's father's voice came from the wheelchair. 'Pull me up, will you, son?'

Robbie put his hands in his father's armpits and lifted him so that he was sitting upright and facing the doctor.

'Sorry, Mr Hanright. How are you feeling?'

'I've been better.'

'Are you in any pain?'

'Nothing out of the ordinary. A bit sick in my stomach but I'm getting used to that.'

'Any irritation on the skin around the stomach at all?'

'Not really.'

'Good, good. Now, as I was saying to your son, you're going to be quite tired in the days to come and it's important that you get plenty of rest. At the same time, a bit of exercise will do you the world of good. Now, when I say exercise, I don't mean anything too strenuous, a bit of gardening perhaps or a short walk around the garden in the evening, that kind of thing.'

The doctor smiled and Robbie's father nodded dismissively without meeting his eye.

'You need to listen to your body. When you're tired, sit down. If you can get someone to help you with the housework and shopping, do that.'

'They're always fussing around me, doctor, you don't need to be encouraging them.'

'What about food? Dad hasn't had much of an appetite this week and he's losing weight from what I can see.'

'Yes, this is a common reaction to radiotherapy, I'm afraid.' He turned to Robbie's father. 'What's the problem exactly? You don't feel hungry?'

'I can't bear the smell of it. Whatever you're putting in my food, Robbie, is turning my stomach. I've never had problems getting food down, doctor, and the only thing that's changed is my chef.'

The consultant laughed.

'You're lucky to have a chef, Mr Hanright,' he said, scribbling something on his pad. 'Here's a prescription for protein powder, just to make sure he's getting enough nutrition.'

John scoffed as Robbie folded the piece of paper and put it in his pocket.

'Righty-o then, that's us for the day. Have you got any questions?'

Robbie looked at his father who had folded his arms and closed his eyes.

'I think we're fine,' Robbie said. 'There's not much more to say, is there?'

'Well, if you have any more questions over the next few weeks, just let me know. You'll have a check-up appointment next week. Otherwise, just make him comfortable and ensure he takes medication if he's in any pain.'

Robbie looked around the office, wanting to take it all in. It was the last station for his father. There was nothing more that could be done to help him and all that was left was to take him home and watch him die. There were various framed certificates on the walls that qualified the consultant to do what he did and a bulging bookcase of reference materials. His window looked across to another wing of the hospital and Robbie could see an old lady propped up in bed with pillows. The consultant had already detached from their meeting and moved on to other things that required his attention on the desk.

'Thank you,' Robbie said.

'It's a pleasure,' he said.

As he wheeled his father through the now-familiar corridors of the hospital, Robbie felt whatever strength had been keeping him going start to give way. With the routine of daily trips to the hospital, conversations with Elizabeth and the busyness of doing something about the cancer, Robbie had been safe. Now that they were leaving behind the pink linoleum floors and sanitised waiting rooms, there would be no daily routine, just a large farmhouse filled with the last breaths of his father. Suddenly he was dogged by all sorts of questions that he should have asked; would his father need help on the toilet? Would he get much worse towards the end? Would he die in pain or quietly in his sleep? The questions collided in his mind and he had to stop walking for a few seconds to catch his breath.

છ

Wendy was sitting on the window ledge at the front of the farmhouse, her trousers rolled up to get the sun on her legs. Robbie rolled his window down to greet his sister in as light a tone as he could muster.

'I've made bread,' she called out, lifting a tea-towelled lump to prove it.

Once in the kitchen, Robbie and Wendy moved about

getting tea ready. When Elizabeth arrived, their father had gone into his bedroom.

'You look tired, Robbie,' Elizabeth said.

'It's been a long week.'

His sisters both smiled and he felt as though whatever happened in the next few weeks would be manageable as long as they were all on the same side.

'I'm thinking about going back to work a few days a week,' Elizabeth said. 'I'm not sure what good it would do to be hanging around here.'

She looked at Robbie and Wendy, the statement hanging in the air for them to challenge.

'Perhaps now is exactly the right time to be hanging around, Lizzie,' Robbie said.

'Why do you say that?'

'Well, put it this way, if you don't hang around now, there will never be another time to do it.'

Elizabeth focused her attention on her fingernails.

'I thought, you know, that knowing he was going to die soon would change the way I felt about him. I thought it would allow me to be more compassionate. I never imagined that he could die with things so unresolved but it looks more and more likely that it will happen.'

'Hold on there, Elizabeth,' Wendy said, sitting next to her at the table. 'Stop talking like he's about to give up the ghost any day now. We've still got lots of time to work things out and allow ourselves to process what lies ahead. Don't we, Robbie?'

The two girls looked at him and the weight of responsibility was once again heavy on his shoulders.

'Sure,' he said.

'See?' She turned back to Elizabeth. 'Don't go back to work yet; spend some time with him. Give him a chance.'

'Another one?'

'Yes, Lizzie, another one.'

The two sisters held hands and Robbie excused himself and went into the living room. Through the window he could see the sun still high in the sky. He would have given anything to be in the newsroom with the lads, laughing beside the photocopier with Niall about his latest outrageous interview with a pseudo-celebrity, or debating a recent rugby match with the sports writers. Robbie's life in Dublin seemed so alluringly simple. The sudden impulse to drink a beer came over him and he grabbed the car keys and stuck his head into the kitchen.

'I'm just nipping out to grab some beer. Be back in ten.'

Avoiding the off licences in Dromore, Robbie went straight to The Cellar in Banbridge with its shelves of dusty wine bottles and extensive range of whiskey. With his head inside the fridge, trying to chisel the ice that had stuck the last six-pack of Stella to the shelf, he did not hear Adam saying hello. After a successful extraction, Robbie spun around and collided with him and his bottle of champagne.

A moment of panic followed as the men tried to grab their alcohol before it hit the ground. The beer was rescued, much to Robbie's delight, and the twelve-year-old single malt was safe in the crook of his elbow but the bottle of champagne broke into pieces and soaked them both. They both stood quietly for several seconds, assessing the damage and wiping their jeans.

'Sorry,' Robbie said.

He could tell that Adam was fighting to remain cool.

'That was the last bottle,' he said.

'I'll get someone to clean this up,' Robbie said, catching the eye of a sales assistant. 'Celebrating something special?'

The light in the off licence was poor but Robbie was almost sure that he saw Adam blushing.

'No, I just fancied something different. I'd better get going. See you later, Robbie.'

He was out the door before Robbie could say another word.

With the bag of alcohol on the passenger seat, Robbie drove

to a small bridge outside town where the Newry Canal towpath crossed the road. He awkwardly propped the six-pack under his cast while he lit a cigarette with his good hand. It was as though the single objective of getting stone cold drunk on a bench beside the river made everything else blend into insignificance. The effort and exhaustion of the last few days had got the better of him and the only place he wanted to be was on that wooden park bench under a sycamore tree, with the noise of the River Bann in the background and a drink in his hand.

It was cold but he didn't care. The temptation to give himself over to self-indulgence and thoughts of 'why me?' was so strong that within minutes he was convinced that he was possibly the most persecuted man in Northern Ireland. The injustice of all those people wanting so much from him made him angry and he threw each empty beer can against the nearest tree with a yell. Glugs of whiskey chased the beer until he was slapping the tree like an impertinent child and cursing everyone he could think of. Why could they not just leave him alone? Why did everyone expect him to pick up the pieces and have all the answers?

With the whiskey bottle half-empty, he began pacing beneath the tree until he was overheated and had to remove his jacket. He was unable to sit still with the thoughts of how hard done by he was playing in his mind. Memories helped to justify his position, mostly of his mother using him as a shield against his father. Nights when John would disappear outside with a bottle of something often ended with fifteen-year-old Robbie being pulled out of bed by his mother in her nightgown and pushed down the stairs with an injunction to, 'sort your father out'. It was no wonder Robbie fell asleep in school. He stamped his fifth can of beer underfoot until it was flat and then threw it like a Frisbee into the river. By the time the whiskey was finished, Robbie was slumped at the bottom of the tree and almost out of cigarettes. Songs were coming to him as he struggled back into his jacket and fixed his collar against the cold.

'Down by the Sally Gardens . . .' he started, tears suddenly catching in his throat. '. . . little snow-white feet. She bid me take love easy . . .' He hummed the forgotten words. '. . . But I was young and foolish, and with her did not agree'.

A cow mooed in the distance and a car backfired on the bridge.

Twenty-One

Robbie woke just in time to see a large black dog squatting only metres from his face. The excrement looked even worse from this angle: lying with his cheek pressed onto the damp wood of the bench, slightly downhill from the animal. Every muscle in his body ached, forcing him to move into a sitting position quite slowly. With a throbbing head and a stomach likely to spill its contents at any moment, Robbie sat upright and took deep breaths of the cool, morning air. The sun was shining weakly through the sycamore branches onto the river and he shuffled along the seat to where he could be warmed by its rays. The walker of the black dog passed him, squatting to lift his dog's deposit and muttering under his breath. Robbie's head was so sore that he couldn't even hang it in shame without feeling as though it were about to roll down his neck and off his shoulders.

The smell of whiskey was strong and caused him to wretch several times before he threw up violently. With a final heave, his stomach was empty and he started to whimper. He was not sure if he would make it to the car, never mind back to the house. After washing his mouth out in the river, he decided to take a short walk along the towpath to sober up. He felt better after vomiting and his thoughts started to order themselves. A slight guilt over last night's maudlin performance was replaced by the realisation that Wendy and Elizabeth were probably worried sick about him. He had not even thought to phone. One of them probably had to stay with his father and would be up now wondering where he had got to.

'I haven't slept a wink all night, Robbie. What on earth happened to you?' Wendy said on the phone.

'I bumped into a few mates in Dromore and went back to one of their houses. Sorry I didn't phone. I'll be home soon.'

Wendy hung up before he had even finished his sentence. He held his phone out in front of him as it started to beep through all the messages and missed calls from the night before. To his right the river frothed and spat beneath the trees, whose branches were interlaced to form a canopy above him. Robbie remembered singing the night before and felt foolish. It was his father's favourite song and he would sing it over and over until his cheeks were wet and his voice hoarse. How drunkenness led to song Robbie did not know. He could not recall a time that his father sang when he was sober. In his early years it was his mother who sang while bread was baking in the oven and all was right with the world. His father would stand outside the kitchen window until she had finished and then say, 'There's none of them can sing so sweet, my singing bird, as you', and she would laugh and send him back to work.

The song became his mantra when he drank late into the night in his work shed. Robbie wondered if his mother ever heard the words floating up from the yard into her bedroom. As a spectator to the death of his parents' love, he knew at the age of ten that he would never be the same again. When his sisters went through phases of dreaming and planning their future romances, Robbie would hear his father's voice in the coal shed. So aware was he of love's ability to die that he never allowed it to live in the first place. After his affair with Joan, he gave very little of himself to the girls he met during his first few years in Dublin. He worked hard, kept a clean home and always maintained complete control of his relationships. Even when

Hannah came along and stuck around so much longer than the others, he still held enough back to be able to make a clean break if necessary.

As Robbie walked to the Terryhoogan lock outside Scarva where the disused canal was shallow and murky, he collected twigs from the hedge. He stopped half-way across it to throw the branches over the edge. Whether he was just hung-over, or in a particularly sentimental mood, he was able to see his marriage a lot more clearly. Hannah was the strong one; she was the one looking after their daughter, alone, in Dublin, while he wasted his time trying to endear himself to a family that resented him. It was his wife who held things together and enabled him to be a functioning adult. How had he not seen it like that before? If only he had asked her to come north with him, she would have known how to get through to Wendy and the best meals to cook for his father. A young woman jogged past him. Robbie sniffed and wiped his eyes with the sleeve of his coat.

'Hello, love,' he said. 'I'm just checking in.'

'Where are you? Can I hear a river?'

Her voice was sleepy and he checked the time on his phone. It was half past seven.

'Yes, I'm out for a walk.'

'Goodness. A bit early for you, isn't it?'

'How's Amy?'

'She's just up. I feel almost human now that she's sleeping better.'

'That's great, love.'

'Robbie?'

'Yes?'

'Are you coming home?'

He bent over and pressed his head against the bridge, willing himself not to cry.

'What are you talking about? Of course I'm coming home.'

'It's just . . . You've been away so long. Don't you miss us?'

'Miss you? Yes, I miss you. You're my family. I don't belong here; I belong with you two in that apartment. I'd come home tomorrow if I could.'

'As long as I know that, you stay as long as you need.'

A mallard duck bobbed in the water beneath the bridge. Robbie stood up straight, squared his shoulders and steadied himself as the blood ran to his head.

'I love you,' Hannah added before hanging up.

ॐ

Back at the house everything was quiet. Wendy had left a brief note saying that she had taken their father out and would be back later. After a shower he felt well enough to pay his mother a visit. Just as he was about to leave the farmhouse, Elizabeth arrived.

'Heavy night?' she said as she brushed past him with shopping bags full of groceries.

'I can explain,' he shouted after her.

'You don't wear that mask of yours very convincingly, brother.'

'Come on, Lizzie, not you too.'

'Oh, I'm sorry. Do you want me to sock you on the arm and say "Good on ya" or something? Don't you think we have enough to worry about without you going AWOL again?'

'I didn't go AWOL. I just went out for a few drinks with some mates. Give me a break.'

'Who?'

'What do you mean?'

'Who did you go out with?'

'Oh, just some mates I bumped into in Dromore.'

'What were their names?'

'Get off my back with the Spanish Inquisition, all right?'

'You're a bloody bad liar, Robbie.'

She shook her head as she unloaded the groceries violently on the table. Robbie collapsed into one of the chairs and held his head in his hands.

'I'm sorry, Lizzie. It all got a bit much.'

She sighed.

'I'll put the kettle on.'

They took their cups of tea out into the orchard where the damson trees blossomed and trumpet-shaped cowslip was at varying stages, from coyly suggesting its presence in the shade, to openly flirting in yellow skirts where the sun shone.

'It's so sad to watch this place go to ruin,' Elizabeth said. 'It would have been nice if it had stayed in the family.'

'Would you have lived here?'

'I would have considered it.'

'It will be weird when it's gone.'

'Very.'

Robbie tried to imagine the new layout, with bungalows stretching from the back fence to the road. With the house flattened and taken away brick by brick, generations of Hanrights would be wiped out.

'I read your article about it,' Elizabeth said quietly.

'You did?'

'And I quote, "We don't buy houses to pass down through the generations any more. We purchase turn key properties in housing developments where all the work has been done for us and we can move out just as easily as we moved in."'

She smiled smugly and Robbie laughed.

'I especially loved the part about how new houses lack the character of their older counterparts and your projection that in years to come we'll have none of the strings or attachments to place that our predecessors had. In a way it sums up your life.'

'It does?'

'Yes. Your lack of attachment to place meant that you could up sticks and move to Dublin. The fact that you've stayed there for so many years suggests that not only have you severed your connections to place, you've also successfully cut your ties to people. Your article was a sort of self-fulfilling prophecy.'

Robbie was stunned not only that his sister followed his articles but also that she had given such an accurate summation of his life.

'I'm a right bollocks, aren't I?'

'You were.'

'You don't think I still am?'

'You came back, didn't you? And I'd go as far to say that in reconnecting with place and people, you've realised the lie that you have been living for far too long.'

'Is that what's going on?' he said lightly, forcing a laugh.

'You're not out of the woods yet,' she said, gentler this time.

'I'm not?'

'When the going gets a little tough, you grab the anaesthetic that you've inherited from your father as quickly as you can.'

He stood up from the low wall on which they had been perching.

'Now wait a minute—'

'No, Robbie, you wait. Am I wrong to guess that you headed off somewhere on your own with a bottle of something and ended up passing out in a ditch? I can see from your face that I'm bang on the money. As if that broken arm wasn't enough. That's twice now since you've been back, isn't it? What you don't realise is that it's not normal to go from caring prodigal son to waking up in an alcohol-induced stupor just like that,' she clicked her fingers and paused. 'It's the product of growing up with an alcoholic father and there's no doubt you suffered the most.'

'Can I just interrupt you there? Where has all this psycho-babble come from all of a sudden? Have you lured me into some sort of therapy with a cup of tea and a biscuit?' He tried to laugh but it came out as more of a scoff.

'I've been seeing someone – a counsellor – for over a year now and it's really helped me. I'm just trying to help you by sharing some of the lessons I've learnt.'

'Sorry to disappoint you, Lizzie, but I'm not asking for your help. Why do all women feel this need to "help" and "fix" us men? We're not like you; we're not into all this "feeling" mumbo jumbo. We're simple creatures who respond to our basic desires and wants. I felt like a beer last night and I went out and had one – no big deal, no hidden code. All right?'

She smiled and he could tell that she was disappointed.

'All right. Sorry, I must have got the wrong end of the stick.'

'Exactly.'

She drained the last of her tea and turned her face towards the sun.

'I'm going to Mum's now if you're not busy and you want to come?' she said, stretching out her legs.

'I was planning on heading over at some stage. I suppose there's no time like the present.'

'She said she had something important to tell me. I never know when to take her seriously, though. She's a bit melodramatic these days. It could be something as mundane as her garden peas being ready or as serious as . . . as . . . '

'That she's pregnant?'

They both laughed and it wasn't until they were walking towards the house that Robbie remembered his run in with Adam the night before. He stopped dead in his tracks and turned to his sister.

'What's wrong? You look like you've seen a ghost.'

'I bumped into Adam last night, quite literally actually.'

'So?'

'He was in the off-licence buying a bottle of champagne.'

Elizabeth's hand flew up to her mouth.

'No,' she said, drawing out the vowel for several seconds.

Robbie shrugged.

'It's probably nothing. They could have just been celebrating his business or something.'

Elizabeth stared at him and then dropped her hand.

'Yes, of course. We're being ridiculous. Don't get all dramatic on me, Robbie.'

'You're telling me.'

Robbie slung his arm around Elizabeth's shoulder as they walked down the yard, running his finger over the cut on the palm of his hand where the glass from the champagne bottle had drawn blood.

Twenty-Two

Robbie thought Elizabeth had not heard the announcement. Except for a brief pause, she continued picking pea pods from the climbers as if nothing had been said. Margaret was sitting on a wooden deck chair in the back garden and had made coffee. The Bodum suddenly captivated Robbie's attention as his mother and Adam studied his face.

'It will seem quite unexpected to you, Robbie, I know,' Adam said from where he stood next to Robbie's mother with his hand on her shoulder.

'No, no, not at all,' Robbie said.

'You think I'm past it, do you?' his mother said, pinching his leg playfully.

'Past it? No, it seems you have discovered a new lease of life since I last saw you.'

'Yes, that's a good way of putting it. A new lease of life.' She looked up at Adam. 'And this man here is to thank for it.'

'Very good.'

'I'm sure it will take a bit of getting used to. It's certainly not conventional.'

'No, certainly not.'

'But we have to do what makes us happy, right?'

'I suppose so.'

'Well Adam makes me happy and I don't care who knows about it. I know those biddies in the town talk about us but

151

that's just because they don't have the guts to get out of their unhappy marriages. They're probably jealous of us.'

Adam nodded.

'You can't choose who you love, can you?'

'No,' Adam said, bending over to kiss her on the cheek. Margaret stretched her bare legs out in front of her. The sun was high in the sky and the absence of wind made it feel like a true summer's day. Adam disappeared inside to get cups from the kitchen.

'I know I've changed a lot since you last saw me,' Margaret said. 'This must all be quite difficult for you but I just want you to know that you don't need to worry. I'm happier now than I ever was and you just have to trust me on that one.'

She patted his leg and turned to Elizabeth.

'Are you so wrapped up in your own little world over there that you didn't hear our news? We're getting married, darling.'

Robbie watched his sister rock back on her heels and gather the pods in a silver colander before standing and turning to face them. The look on her face was impossible to decipher.

'Lizzie?' their mother said. 'I thought you'd be excited.'

'You're still married, Mum,' she said quietly, pressing the plunger down on the coffee pot.

'Well . . .'

Adam reappeared. 'We have tried to sort that out but John refuses to sign the papers.'

'So what will you do?' Elizabeth asked.

'Well, there's no law to stop us getting engaged. We'll work out the finer details in time but I couldn't wait any longer,' Adam said.

'Well, what can I say? Congratulations.'

She hugged her mother first and then Adam. Robbie stood up and moved in to shake Adam's hand and give his mother a kiss on the cheek. When Elizabeth had poured four cups of coffee, they toasted the couple's future happiness. Margaret was giddy from the confession and filled any gap in their conversation with inane details about her relationship with Adam, their ideas for the wedding and anything else that sprung to her mind.

'Oh, and I was thinking, Robbie. By the time a date is set, Amy will be walking. She could be our flower girl.'

'Hmm?'

'A flower girl, at the wedding – do you think Hannah would agree to it? I never thought I'd get to have another wedding and it'll be just how I'd always dreamed, without Granny's interference. I wanted a flower girl then, remember I told you, Adam? Well, anyway, she wouldn't hear of it.'

Elizabeth reached out to put her hand on Robbie's shoulder and announced that they had to go. After arranging to take his mother to Sainsbury's the next day when Adam was away, Robbie collapsed into the passenger seat of Elizabeth's car.

'Well, there you are,' he said as they pulled out of the driveway. 'I'll bet you didn't see that coming?'

Elizabeth laughed.

'If you'd been here the last few years and watched how Mother has made the impossible possible time and time again, you wouldn't be so flabbergasted now.'

'I was wondering why you weren't flipping out back there.'

'I honestly don't think I have the energy for our family any more. Have you ever heard the like of it?'

'Everyone thinks their family is crazier than the next.'

'Well, do you know anyone else whose mother is marrying a car mechanic five years her junior when she should be playing Bingo and drinking tea with her widowed friends?'

'They looked at one another and started to laugh until they cried. Elizabeth stopped the car, gripped the steering wheel and threw her head back while Robbie tried to catch his breath. Each time their laughter died down, one of them would start to giggle and set them both off again. Neither rolling down the car window, nor slapping one another on the arm could stop the hysteria and it was not until a tractor chugged past and blared its horn that the two could sober up.

They were parked on the quiet Blackskull Road and a flock of geese came in to land on a large pool of water that had formed in the bottom of one of the fields. Robbie and Elizabeth watched the birds as they skidded on the wet grass, attempted to dive beneath the pool's shallow surface and started to fight with one another out of frustration. Robbie took his sister's hand and they stayed that way until the tractor passed by again and the driver shook his fist at them.

༅

Wendy's reaction to the news was less than positive. After settling her grumbling father into the armchair in the living room, she appeared in the doorway of the spare bedroom where Robbie and Elizabeth had decided to start going through some of the rubbish that had accumulated there.

Their mother had called the room Narnia when the children were younger and joked that it was possible to get lost for days among the odds and ends that had been gathering dust for generations. The room had three outside walls, which made it impossible to keep warm in the winter. The ceiling slanted from the door downwards and the light bulb, which had blown years before, had never been replaced. Robbie and Elizabeth used an extension cord to bring a bedside lamp into the room and were tucked away in a corner with a box of their childhood toys when Wendy interrupted them.

'Look what we found, Wendy,' Elizabeth said. 'Come over here to the light.'

Elizabeth held out a small, toy monkey that had gathered so much dust, its fur was more grey than brown. Wendy did not speak as she fingered the toy, lifting its small plastic thumb to fit in the hole that was designed for its mouth.

'Monkey,' she finally said.

'They're all here. I had no idea Mum had kept them all.'

Wendy hovered above them, watching as Elizabeth lifted one toy after another from the box and snatching the ones that were hers.

'It feels like so long ago,' she said.

'Let's not work out how long ago,' Robbie said. 'It would only depress us.'

'What are we supposed to do with all this?' Wendy said, scanning the mountains of unwanted things around them.

'We were talking about it earlier and decided that there is no time like the present to sort it all out,' Robbie said.

'Besides,' Elizabeth added, 'there might be some stuff we'd want to keep.'

Wendy sighed.

'Sorry, but I don't have time for this. I'll have to leave it to you two. I'm exhausted after the afternoon I've had with Dad. We only drove to Ballynahinch for ice cream and back but you'd think I'd taken him to a torture chamber given the way he complained. He didn't even eat the ice cream; his appetite is completely ruined.'

'They warned us about that.'

'And he still looks yellow to me.'

In the poor lighting, it looked to Robbie as though someone had placed their hands on either side of Wendy's face and pulled the skin until it hung like the jowls of a turkey around her neck. Her clothes had the remnants of their father's ice cream on them and her eyes looked as though they would be much happier closed. With her hands on her hips, she stood above him and Elizabeth and seemed like a formidable character. Robbie struggled to think of a time when she had soft edges and a less volatile temperament.

'We need to tell you something,' he said as she turned to leave.

'What?'

'You might like to sit down.'

'For God's sake, Robbie, just spit it out. I don't have time for this.'

'Adam and Mum are getting married.'

Her hand went immediately to her chest and there was a sharp intake of breath. Out of the corner of his eye he could see Elizabeth looking at him but he kept watching Wendy, frozen and surrounded by junk.

There was a large crash as she pushed a box of old newspapers to the ground. Robbie and Elizabeth watched in horror as she lashed out at the things around her; kicking the wheels of an old pram, spilling the contents of a bag of Christmas decorations and tearing a path through the mounds of old coats, sun-bleached curtains and picnic blankets until she reached the far wall and there was nowhere else to go. She slid down the wall and collapsed in a heap on the floor as the dust settled. They could hear their father calling up to them from the living room but when he stopped there was no noise except for Wendy's laboured breathing. Hidden from view by several large boxes, Robbie and Elizabeth sat silently. She had tears in her eyes and he was gripping a stuffed bumblebee so hard that its eyes were bulging and his knuckles white. Wendy's quiet sobs carried across the room, soon joined by Elizabeth's and the eerie out-of-tune melody of a jewellery box.

Twenty-Three

John's colour did not improve, nor did his appetite but he complained less and less of being in pain and the family soon settled into a rhythm of care. Elizabeth arrived every morning to have breakfast with Robbie and John, then the three of them took a short walk around the garden if the weather was clear. This soon became Robbie's favourite part of the day. Despite his father's protestations that the eggs were overcooked or that the garden was in a state, he soon settled down and accepted Elizabeth's arm. Father and daughter rarely spoke to one another directly, tending to address their statements to Robbie instead. He felt as though his being there was making space for something to happen that otherwise would not.

After their stroll around the garden, Elizabeth would make tea while Robbie settled his father in bed again. He rarely slept through the night and was often tired by mid-morning. For the few hours that he slept, Robbie and Elizabeth disappeared into Narnia to separate the contents of the room into 'KEEP' and 'THROW' piles. This was often a time-consuming task as they picked apart their past in the form of old photograph albums, cases of cassette tapes and hand-me-down clothes.

A bag full of marbles could set them back half an hour as they found out if Robbie was still unbeatable. The dog-eared rocking horse had to be sat on as they debated whether or not Robbie's daughter would enjoy it if he could fix it up a bit. One lunchtime they took sandwiches and tea into the room and sat for an hour passing photographs between them, laughing at old haircuts and remembering the names of relatives dead and gone. Sorting through the remnants of their family history gave them a sense of purpose. At the end of each day, they had something to show for themselves, be it only a dusted and orderly album that could be kept in remembrance of their father's aunts and uncles who had once lived at Larkscroft Farm.

For Robbie, the task kept him focused on something over which he had some control. With his father's condition relatively stable, he was able to enjoy Elizabeth's company, drink a lot of tea and dust the soil off the roots of his past to see just how deep they really went. His days were simple and productive and he felt better than he had in a long time.

In the evenings Wendy came round, phoning before she left home to see if it would suit to bring her children. Robbie had not mentioned her separation but took the time to play with the boys in the front field until night started to fall and they could no longer see the football.

Despite the relative calm that had settled on the farmhouse, and no matter how hard they tried to act normally, it was impossible to ignore the sense of death that stubbornly persisted. Robbie hated when his sisters left for the evening and he was alone in the house with his father. Often he would listen outside the door to his breathing and once or twice had sneaked in when it slowed. Every morning he would wake up with a start, worrying that his father might have died in the night. Then he would hear him clearing his throat or shouting for Robbie to do something.

It was a Friday morning when Robbie woke to the sound of his father's wailing. The previous night they had discussed the possibility of going on a day trip and John had surprised them all by suggesting they take the ferry across Strangford Lough to visit the National Trust property on the peninsula. As Robbie went down the stairs two at a time, he thought of the rhododendron in bloom and the water lilies like cupped hands on the surface of the lake. He found his father in a heap in the bathroom after he had slid down the radiator and burnt his left hand. There were tears in his eyes.

'Don't panic, Dad,' he said, his voice calm. 'I'll get you back into bed and ring the doctor.'

His father's medicine was organised in a large plastic pillbox on the kitchen counter. The digestive enzymes were kept in the fridge but the rest of the multi-coloured tablets were labelled and stored in little compartments. They had said no to morphine after being told how addictive it was; Robbie now wished he had taken some for back-up. While his father swallowed painkillers, Robbie was advised to bring him into hospital immediately.

'I'm sorry to say that the cancer has spread,' the oncologist announced later that afternoon. He and Robbie were standing in a small room down the hall from his father's ward.

'I see.'

'It has metastasised into his lungs and the cancer cells are in his bloodstream. That's all we can tell at the moment and there's not a lot of point doing any more tests.'

He looked down at his shoes and then back at Robbie.

'We advise family members at this time to make the patient comfortable in a hospice or at home, whichever route you have decided to take.'

'Right.'

'Patients can often deteriorate quite quickly at this stage.'

'How quickly?'

He shrugged.

'You may only have a few days.'

The consultant left the room and Robbie watched as the city came to life below. Shop owners on the Lisburn Road opened their shutters and nurses and doctors walked across the car park with briefcases and lunch bags slung over their shoulders.

Apart from one bed that had the curtain pulled round it, his father was the only person on the ward. He had drips attached to his arm and a mask over his face.

'What's all this for?' Robbie asked a nurse who was fiddling with a tube.

'This one is to control the pain, this one is saline fluid to keep him hydrated and he's getting some oxygen from the mask.'

'Thank you.'

The image of his father so thin and breathless on the bed was disturbing. His fingers twitched at his side and one had a probe attached to it. Robbie took his time to pull up a chair and watched his father's chest rising and falling slowly.

'I'm right here, Dad,' he said quietly, resting his hand on his father's arm. He sat like that until his sisters arrived, bleary-eyed and frightened.

'I don't understand,' Elizabeth began. 'I thought we had more time. He's been so strong this last while.'

Robbie picked at a loose thread on his t-shirt and focused on the people walking in and out of the coffee shop across the road. Despite the promise of summer, the girls still wore their coats.

'Do we have options?' Wendy asked.

'Not at this stage, no,' replied Robbie solemnly .

Elizabeth sat down and started crying into her scarf. Wendy did not move; Robbie wondered if she had even blinked.

'We need to make some decisions about whether we want him in a hospice or not.'

'Absolutely not,' Wendy said, shuddering to life with the suggestion. 'I hate those places and you can rest assured that he'd hate it even more. No, it won't do.'

'I don't know if we're fit to look after him,' Robbie said.

'We'll just have to be. He stays at Larkscroft and that's final. It's going to be a tough time for us all,' she said, putting a hand on Elizabeth's shoulder.

ಬಂ

Several days later, when John and Robbie arrived back at the house, Robbie smiled at what Elizabeth had done to their father's bedroom in his absence. The windows had been opened to get rid of the stale smell and the curtains pushed back to allow the morning sun into the room. Large bunches of fresh flowers sat in vases beside his bed and everything was clean and tidy. His father had been heavily sedated for the journey but he woke long enough in the afternoon to take a good look at his surroundings.

'Where am I?' he rasped.

Robbie had been sitting in an armchair in the corner where the last of the sunlight was shining. Unsure of whether his father was hallucinating from the pain medication or not, Robbie helped to prop him up on the pillows so he could get a better look around the room.

'You're in the spare room, Dad.'

'What's all this bloody stuff then?' he said, sweeping his hand feebly towards the new box of tissues Elizabeth had put beside his bed and the bowl of fresh fruit that she had washed and arranged that morning.

'It's just some things that Lizzie thought might brighten up the room,' he said quietly, not wanting her to overhear.

John narrowed his eyes and his head fell back on the pillow.

'What happened? My memory is not co-operating with me this morning.'

'You had to go into hospital yesterday after you fell in the bathroom—'

'I didn't fall in the bathroom, I remember that much. I just needed to sit down and there was nothing for me to sit on.'

'Well anyway, I took you to the hospital—'

'Yes, yes, I remember all that, for goodness sake.'

'They did some tests,' Robbie said, wishing that someone else could have the conversation with his father.

'Judging by all this, it didn't go that well,' his father said, looking up at the drips surrounding his bed.

'No.'

Any conversation that followed centred on John's small sphere of influence at the farm: was the cow getting milked? Had the pigeon decoy been constructed? Was the oil running low? Did the yard need sweeping?

His enquiries were the summation of his interest in life, together with passing remarks about the weather or casual references to the changing light of the season. Robbie had wheeled the television into his room and his father spent most of the day watching it and coughing little bits of phlegm into a bowl at his bedside. Nurses came and went to give him bed baths, change his clothes and fiddle with his drips while Elizabeth wandered in and out with cups of tea, which he never drank.

&

It wasn't until Robbie heard a car start up that he knew his mother had been to the house. She had parked on the road but Robbie pulled back the curtains in time to see her bright blue Citroën Saxo drive off with the exhaust smoke thick in the air behind it. He lay down to try and untangle the remnants of his dream from the image of his mother's car disappearing up Quilly Road as the sun was beginning its ascent. The cow mooed in the yard. Robbie groaned and braced himself for the cold before pulling his clothes on as quickly as possible.

When Robbie pressed his ear against his father's door on the way to the bathroom, he could just make out his breathing. At least she had left him alive. It was six o'clock. There was no trace of his mother except the faint lingering smell of perfume in the hallway. Wearing Wellington boots, a coat and a hat, Robbie set about his morning tasks somewhat distracted by the mystery of his parents' reunion.

If Wendy was right, his parents had not been alone together

since the day four years ago when she had walked out of the farmhouse. It was his father's greatest embarrassment that Margaret had never returned and that she was actually happier without him. Within the year she had moved into a lovely house, taken up pottery and secured a job in the office at the hardware shop in Dromore. What did he make of her working? From the age of twenty-two when she got married, she had stayed at home. Hearing that she answered the phones at a shop where men came in wearing their work-clothes, must have given him quite a shock. Perhaps he phoned to find out if it were true and then hung up when he heard her voice. Would he have been intrigued by the woman he was married to for twenty-eight years who had taken on an entirely new identity?

With a quarter of a bucket full of milk at his feet and the imposing body of the heifer above him, Robbie tried to imagine what business she would have had with his father. Had she come to make her peace, offer a few kindly words of goodbye before he passed on, or was it more sinister than that? Had she decided to say all the things she could never admit when they were married? She might have stored it all up, hidden the words under her tongue until that very moment. As much as Robbie would not have blamed his mother if the latter was true, he somehow knew that it was not. She was content now; secure in the new place she had made for herself in the world. Robbie hoped that she had come to pass on some of the peace she had found. He slapped the hindquarters of the cow so that it waddled into the paddock, and carried the milk pail down to the house.

'Well, Dad, how are we this morning?' Robbie said, trying to balance a tray of breakfast and close the door with his elbow at the same time. His father regarded him with suspicion.

'The cow's milked, tea wet and I cooked your eggs the way you like them.'

'I'm not hungry.'

'You didn't touch your dinner last night and you haven't even looked at the eggs.'

'I said I'm not hungry.'

Robbie ignored him and set about clearing a space on his father's bedside table for the food. Wendy had bought a knee tray with a beanbag beneath it so that it moulded itself around his legs and did not move. Robbie set it on top of his father who wriggled under the weight. When Robbie went to lift the plate of eggs across, his father kicked out and sent the entire lot into the air, onto the walls and down on top of them both. Robbie stood completely still while the eggs wobbled on the bedspread and the plate rolled across the carpet.

'I said I wasn't hungry.'

'Well, Dad, if that changes, you'll know where to find something to eat,' Robbie said and turned to leave the room. When Elizabeth arrived an hour later, she went straight in to see her father.

'What on earth is wrong with him this morning?'

'Don't ask me.'

'Well I'm asking you because I'm sure the cold egg all over the place wasn't entirely down to Dad.'

'The fact that is cold and all over the place is entirely down to Dad. If things had gone according to my plan, he would have eaten it when I brought it to him, which was when it was still hot and on the plate.'

Robbie was reading through a stack of old comics they had come across the day before in Narnia. He was still in his pyjamas and an old dressing gown on which he had spilt the milk from his cereal. Elizabeth sighed.

'Don't take it personally. He's just got no appetite.'

'I'm not taking it personally.'

'Ok. His mood seems very low today. Do you think there's any chance of getting him out of bed?'

'Dunno.'

'Oh come on, get a grip on yourself.'

'Leave me alone.'

'Sitting here in your pyjamas in the middle of the day because our dying father didn't like your eggs,' she said, laughing. 'It's ridiculous.'

Throwing the magazine on the floor, Robbie gathered the belt of his dressing gown and left the room. He could hear his sister shouting after him, something about being a petulant child. After phoning Hannah and hearing the daily rundown on how their daughter had slept the night before, he showered and got dressed. By the time he went in to see his father, Elizabeth had cleaned up the remains of his breakfast and Robbie was more composed.

'Fancy a walk, Dad?' he asked.

From the grunt that his father exacted, it was clear that his mood had not improved throughout the morning.

'Something to eat?'

He had slipped down in the bed and Robbie could see that he was straining his neck to watch the television.

'Can I help you sit up a bit better?'

His father turned from the television as though his son was a great inconvenience and fixed his eyes on him.

'That cow needs selling.'

'The cow?'

'You know, the big black and white animal that you're meant to be milking every day. You need to sell it.'

'Right.'

Robbie turned his attention to the flowers at his father's bedside and started fluffing them as though they were a pillow.

'Do you know how?'

'C'mon, Dad, you don't need to be worrying about all this now. I'll sort it out.'

'It's my cow and I want you to sell it.'

'Fine, I'll do it.'

'How?'

'You know, I'll find someone who wants to buy a cow, Gumtree or something.'

'Who's that?'

'Never mind.'

'You'll go up to Billy Plumber's place and ask for the lend of his trailer. Get it tonight if you can—'

'Tonight? But I'm—'

'Tonight, Robbie. The market's tomorrow.'

'Fine.'

'Tomorrow lunchtime get some hay into the trailer, coax the cow in and then be over in Markethill for four to get her loaded off and registered. She won't fetch much, but make sure she's good and clean before she goes.'

'Right you are.'

His father fell back into the bed and returned his gaze to the television. Robbie loitered beside him for a few minutes but it was clear that his father had nothing more to say.

Twenty-Four

Robbie enlisted Adam to help him coax the cow into the back end of Billy Plumber's trailer. He had to sneak him round the back of the house so as not to offend his father, but it would have been impossible to get the cow into the trailer alone. The plan was never to take Adam to the market but when he jumped into the passenger seat of Billy's Land Rover, Robbie didn't consider asking him to get out.

They were both covered in sweat and laughing. Adam had narrowly avoided a grass-covered hoof hitting him in the groin and Robbie had spent several awkward moments trying to worm his way out of the trailer once the cow was inside. Robbie's grubby jeans and Wellingtons were a far cry from the sharp suits and designer shoes he wore in Dublin, and a journey to the cattle market to sell his father's cow was the last thing he had envisaged doing while the old man was dying. But in the midst of Adam's chatter about a garden show he went to with Margaret, Robbie found himself relaxing.

The back roads to Markethill peaked and troughed across the countryside as fields of barley shimmered in the afternoon sun. He felt so comfortable on the corners, remembering the lie of the land as if he had driven it yesterday. When he slowed to overtake a woman and her daughter who were riding their horses on the lane, Robbie could remember the exact spot where his car had gone off the road in the snow. He related the accident to Adam: coming round the corner too fast, trying to use his gears to slow down on the hill and remembering the awful moment when the wheels locked and the car careened into Mrs. Dempsey's front fence.

He did not mention the way Joan had screamed and how Mrs. Dempsey had made her hot tea with sugar; or the way his mind raced to think of something he could tell Martin that would explain why he and Joan were in the car together so far from home but Adam must have picked something up from his silence.

'You have so many memories here.'

'Yes, I do.'

'It must be hard to live so far away from your home.'

'It's not that bad. I've a great life in Dublin.'

'Quite different,' he said, pointing his thumb towards the trailer behind them.

Robbie looked at Adam.

'Yes actually.'

'My family are from County Down. My parents are dead and I was an only child. Sometimes I wish I could tell them about the life I have now, although my father would find it difficult to understand some of my choices. He was a minister.'

'It is hard to have a good relationship with your parents.'

Adam laughed and slapped Robbie's thigh.

'Yes, you know all about that.'

When they arrived at the market, there was a queue of similar trucks with trailers from the entrance up the street. It moved quickly and within minutes Robbie was at the front. He made several attempts to reverse the trailer into the offloading bay before one of the staff members knocked on his window.

'Need some help?' he said and Robbie heard his friend sniggering in the background.

Robbie wound the window back up and straightened up for the fourth attempt. Drivers in the queue were straining their necks to see what the hold-up was but Robbie managed to lodge the back end of the trailer at the entrance to the market. The men opened the gate and drove the cow into a stall inside. After filling in the relevant forms, Robbie and Adam had twenty minutes to kill before the auction. They found a chip shop on the main street and sat on a bench outside to eat.

'Most Friday nights when I was young we got a battered sausage and chips from the town,' Robbie said, licking the salt off his lips.

'Your mother still does.'

Robbie turned to face him.

'Really?'

Adam nodded and speared several chips onto his fork at a time.

'And every week she tells me about the chippie on Maypole Hill that was destroyed in a chip pan fire.'

'That's right,' Robbie said, pulling his collar up against the wind. 'What about your Mini?'

'I'm nearly there.'

'Good man.'

'These long evenings are great for getting work done.'

They watched a group of teenagers moving slowly up the street towards the chip shop. The boys had their hoods up and walked with their arms entangled in the coats of young girls. Their language was foul and their pace slow; Robbie tried to guess their age. They were too young to pull off the cigarettes cupped in their palms and yet their faces looked as though they had seen far too much to be in their early teens. The girls had black eye make-up smudged around their eye sockets, which looked as though it had been there for weeks. Their tight jeans squeezed the fat from their stomachs over their waistbands like excess glue. Yet something about their unity and the aimless way they seemed to be spending their evening appealed to Robbie.

'Wasn't it great to be young?' he said.

Adam laughed.

'Are you kidding? I hated being a teenager. I spent my free time doing chores while my mother counselled women from the congregation in our front room. All the other kids were out doing whatever kids did at that age, but not me.'

Robbie imagined all the work his mother did while he spent evenings in Dromore with his friends. On more than one occasion he came home drunk and his mother had the job of cleaning up his vomit. Imagining what she must have thought of him then ruined his appetite.

'I was a selfish child,' Robbie said, offering his leftover chips to Adam.

'Perhaps you were but there's no point beating yourself up, is there?'

'I don't know; it makes me feel a bit better.'

He stood up before Adam could respond and walked to the corner to check on the market.

'C'mon we'll head down there – see if there's any movement.'

An hour later, with £160 in his pocket and an empty trailer, Robbie headed home as Adam hummed a tune beside him. Neither spoke as they raced the sunset, anxious to get the truck back to Billy. His mother's house was on the way and he pulled over at the end of the road for Adam to get out.

'Good man, Robbie.'

'Thanks for your help.'

'That's what I'm here for.'

He shrugged when he spoke and seemed so harmless. Robbie smiled and waved goodbye.

❧

Robbie tiptoed into the room to reduce the volume on the television and jumped when his father spoke.

'I've been lying here trying to work you out,' John said, struggling to push himself into a sitting position.

'Dad, I thought you were sleeping.' Robbie clicked on his bedside light. 'What do you mean?'

'What are you doing here, in Northern Ireland?'

Robbie looked over his shoulder: the door was open behind him and he considered leaving.

'Don't be daft. I came because you're sick.'

'And that's it, is it?'

'Why else would I be here?'

His father screwed up his face and hit Robbie when he attempted to make him more comfortable.

'Sit down,' he said.

Robbie had often wakened in the night and imagined some sort of bedside conversation between himself and his father. All the emotional complexity of their relationship would be ironed out between them, with father apologising, son explaining. In some imaginings his father would call himself a 'cunt' and Robbie would agree but then humbly acknowledge that it was all water that had passed under the bridge and everyone had turned out all right. He had imagined tears, hand-holding and near-death whispers of regret for the loss Robbie and his siblings had experienced in their childhood. That was before Robbie knew that the farm had been sold to the Johnsons. He knew that inheriting a farmhouse would never begin to make up for the ways his father had let him down but it would have been better than nothing.

'I saw that O'Shea girl come looking for you.'

Robbie slowly lowered himself into the armchair beside his father's bed.

'Oh you did, did you?'

'That girl's trouble and you know it.'

'She was just saying hello.'

'Where did youse go?'

'You were spying on me?'

'I've got little else to do all day.'

'What does it matter to you anyway?'

His father's hands were twitching by his side and his jaundice looked worse in the lamplight.

'I just don't see why you want to be bothering with the likes of her again.'

Robbie looked at the carpet and thought for one awful moment that he might cry. His father stuttered beside him.

'I . . . I . . . I might not have said anything at the time, but them pair were bad news.'

The gong for the ten o'clock news sounded in the background and Robbie turned to see a sharp-suited young man organising his papers on the news desk. He was suddenly aware of his own breathing, fast and frantic compared to his father's slow and laboured inhalations.

'I've been doing a bit of thinking today.' He took a moment to clear his throat. 'Some things have been made clear to me, let's just say. I wasn't what you would call a model father. Now I had my reasons, mind you, but even so.'

Robbie had composed himself enough to be able to look at his father.

'What I'm trying to say is . . . Well, just seeing that woman again, it made me think about how far you've come, that's all.'

His father sank back in the bed, his chest heaving from the effort of speaking more than he had in months.

'All right, Dad. That's all in the past.'

John nodded, suddenly impatient for the conversation to be over. Patting the bedclothes for the remote control, he turned the volume up on the television and Robbie left the room.

'What was all that about?' Elizabeth said when he joined her on the sofa.

She and Wendy had opened a bottle of wine.

'Joan came to see me last week.'

His siblings looked at one another. Wendy set her glass on the table and Robbie thought she might leave. Instead, she lifted the bottle of wine and poured some into a third glass before handing it to Robbie.

'That's a blast from the past,' she said, lifting her glass up again and settling back into the chair. Elizabeth took her lead from Wendy, sitting back and waiting for Robbie to explain.

'Remember that day we went to the garden show?'

His sisters nodded.

'I saw her that day.'

'I knew you were acting weird. Didn't I say that, Lizzie?' Wendy said.

'Yeah, you did.'

'She wants to talk everything through.'

'Do you?' Wendy asked quietly.

Robbie looked from her to Elizabeth and then at the wall.

'No, I don't see the point in dragging it all up. I've spent so long trying to forget.'

'You can't though, can you?' asked Elizabeth.

'I have my own family to worry about – that's what I told her.'

'You should do it,' Wendy's voice came quietly from the other side of the room.

'What?' Robbie said. 'Is all this not enough for me to deal with right now?'

'You're talking about our dad dying? Her kids were only this big when their dad was shot for trying to uncover the dirty things that go on in this country. I dunno, I just . . . I suppose I feel for her kids.'

The room was quiet, except for the low hum of their father's television in the background. Robbie thought of his two nephews, their blond hair and often-dirty faces. He watched his elder sister swilling the wine around her glass and saw that the hardness that was once so deep around her eyes had turned to soft lines of grief. When she looked at him, it was painful to hold her gaze.

'Dad knows about this?' Wendy asked.

'He saw her picking me up outside.'

She nodded.

'What did you tell him?'

'I said it was all in the past and not to worry himself.'

'Good.'

'So are you going to see her?' Elizabeth asked.

Robbie drained the contents of his glass and ran his fingers through his hair.

'I don't know. I don't know anything any more. My life has gone from being incredibly simple to painfully complex in the space of a month. There were so many more loose ends waiting for me here than I had imagined. I can't even begin to think about going back down that road again, but I owe it to Joan, you know? It wasn't just you lot that I left behind all those years ago.'

Elizabeth topped up their wine glasses.

'You're doing the right thing,' she said and Wendy agreed.

He wanted to hug them but instead focused on a speck of dirt on his trouser leg, rubbing it until it had long disappeared and his finger was hot.

Twenty-Five

Robbie took the Blackskull Road to Joan's house. She had the end terrace in a row of five. They were built from the same brick with awnings over the front step. Joan had called it 'posh' when they had first moved in. Martin and she had bought it when they had moved back from Monaghan and she was pregnant with her second child. There were nothing but fields and country lanes surrounding the houses, which looked as though they had been cut and pasted out of a housing estate and did not belong there.

Robbie got out of the car and, instead of walking towards the house, headed for a small bridle path about twenty metres down the road. During one of their few heart-to-hearts, Martin had described the sunset from the gate at the top of the lane overlooking his house. The image had never left Robbie of his boss balanced on a farmer's gate looking down on his family home as the sun went down.

When Robbie uncovered the gate beneath years of weed growth it was rusted through and had broken free from its hinge at the top. Disappointed, he pushed it open and looked around for somewhere to sit. The row of houses was small at the bottom of the hill and Robbie could see that the clouds on the horizon were going to block any sign of the sunset. He dug his hands into his pockets and tried to picture Martin there.

Although Martin was such a significant figure in his younger years, Robbie had tried to forget him when he moved to Dublin. In the early days of working in the Republic, Robbie would have remembered a joke or funny story that Martin had told him but would refuse to share it with new friends for fear of keeping his memory alive. Martin's big hands, the way he frowned when he concentrated, his bad language and his ability to be in the right place at the right time with the right questions were only a few of the things that came back to him.

It was not difficult to paint a physical picture of Martin – he always wore the same thing: a faded black t-shirt, black jeans and brown boots. His coat was a hand-me-down from a dead uncle; a good waxed Barbour raincoat the colour of pine needles. Robbie could just picture him lighting a cigarette in the armpit of his jacket while the rain drizzled about him.

He rubbed together the palms of his hands before getting to his feet and taking a deep breath of country air. The fields were parcelled up and pale, with sheep dotted across them, flanked by lambs unsteady on their feet.

'Well I'll be . . .' Joan said at the door. She was drying her hands on a tea towel and had something red spilt down the front of her blouse. 'You've arrived at a bad time.' She looked over her shoulder towards the kitchen where a young girl was yelling at someone out of sight.

'I need to talk to you,' he said. 'Please.'

'Go in there and give me five minutes,' she said, motioning with the end of her tea towel to the front room.

After closing the door behind him, Robbie heard her pad down the hallway and shout over the top of her daughters' argument. The room was different from how he remembered it. The furniture may have been the same but bright throws covered the sofas and something akin to sarongs hung over the coffee table and television stand. Ornaments gawked at him from the mantelpiece: a collection of china ladies pushing prams, several figurines of ballerinas perfectly poised and a few misplaced trophies of men with footballs. He sank deep into a single chair in the corner and waited for Joan to settle her children. Several minutes later he heard her in the hallway.

'Sorry to keep you. I've got the kettle on, if you want a cuppa?'

She had tried to get the stains out of her top, leaving wet patches with smeared pink centres.

'I'm ok, thanks.'

When she sat on the edge of the sofa, Robbie noticed that she still had the tea towel in her hand.

'This isn't easy for me,' he began, at once appalled that his throat was closing over and his eyes had begun to ache from the effort of holding back tears. Joan went to speak and he stopped her with his hand and took a deep breath.

'I treated you so badly. I didn't mean to.' He laughed. 'There I go again. It's never my fault, is it?'

Robbie stood up and started pacing.

'I wanted to apologise. When you came to see me the other day I was dismissive and I'm sorry. It's not just that, though. I'm sorry for all of it.'

'You were young. . .' Joan said. She was staring at the ground and Robbie coughed to ease the pressure in his throat.

'No, Joan. I was old enough to know better,' he said, kneeling in front of her.

She looked at him as though she was waiting for him to take back the apology. The wooden floor made kneeling quite painful and Robbie felt foolish. He was unsure whether he should take her hand or get up and give her some space.

'My goodness,' she said, discovering the tea towel and using it to dab the corners of her eyes. 'I wasn't expecting that. I've spent the last five years feeling guilty and angry. I don't want to be like that any more. It's not fair on the girls.'

Robbie shuffled backwards until he could pull himself onto the armchair.

'You're not the one who should feel guilty,' he said.

The sun had all but disappeared, and the room felt as though it was shrinking as dusk snuck in and settled in the corners. At first her tears rolled silently down her cheeks but soon they caused her entire body to convulse and, as hard as she tried to show restraint, her crying took on a life of its own as she buried her face in a cushion. Robbie, paralysed by uncertainty, looked on as she pounded the arm of the sofa with her fist. They stayed like that for several minutes, she sobbing into the settee and he watching helplessly from the sidelines. After a while the sobs turned to moans and gradually faded to hiccups as she tried to find a dry spot on her tea towel.

'I'm sorry,' she said, blowing her nose. 'I just never thought this day would come. Losing Martin was awful, devastating if I'm honest, but you made it so much worse.'

Her attention was focused on the tea towel again.

'They were going to take the kids off me. I was this close to losing them,' she said, measuring an invisible distance between her thumb and first finger. 'You just left. I couldn't believe it. I kept waiting for you to ring or send a letter. I even imagined you showing up on the doorstep.'

She laughed.

'You were the only one who could have understood. No one else got it. All I wanted was to talk about it. I just wanted to talk.'

Robbie had been picking at a loose bit of thread on the throw covering his chair.

'I don't know what else to say,' he said.

Joan looked at him and he could see that in spite of his best effort, she was still disappointed.

'Thank you for coming to see me,' she said. 'I have something upstairs for you. I'll be right back.'

When she left the room, he took to pacing the floor and tugging at the bottom of his pullover.

Joan reappeared with a small envelope.

'It's from Martin,' she said. 'I never opened it.'

'For me?'

'Yep.'

'But . . .'

'I suppose he knew you better than you knew yourself.'

Robbie took it from her and she squeezed his hand as they touched.

'I'll be off then,' he said, scooping his coat from the arm of the chair. 'I'll be around for a few more weeks.'

She nodded.

As he got into the car he could just see the last of the sunset in a thick strip of sky between the cloud and the horizon, red and glowering just as Martin had described.

∞

Robbie,

They say you should keep your friends close and your enemies closer. You have been both friend and enemy, as well as the closest thing I have to a son. I hope you never have to read this letter but the chances are you will. Joan is a strong woman and she will be fine but I don't want my daughters growing up rough. Look out for them and make sure they know I kept their photos on my desk. You're still young but you'll do well. Don't let anyone tell you otherwise.

Martin

He had pulled over on a small country lane and, because the light inside the car was broken, Robbie read the letter bent over his headlights. The alarm was pinging that his car door was ajar, so he re-read Martin's words quickly and got back into the vehicle. He held the envelope tightly, then swore loudly and banged the steering wheel.

When he felt the tears, Robbie started laughing and rocking in his seat, full of the anxiety of a man unaccustomed to being overcome. The radio was on but with no signal in the country, the static did little to fill the silence. As he wriggled his toes, he felt an urge to throw something and watch it break into little pieces. He looked around him but it was pitch black and the only things he could find in the back seat were banana peels and an open sports bag, the contents of which had overflown the footwell.

By the light of a match, he rummaged in his boot and found his father's record player that he had put there with the intention of taking it into town to get a new needle. It looked more like a small suitcase with catches on its front and a wooden handle with which to wind it. The wood was smooth and smelt of furniture polish. One minute he was running his hand over it, the next punching it until forced to withdraw his fist and shake it to stop the throbbing.

With a cry of frustration, he grabbed it by the handle and walked into the middle of the road where the light from his headlights stretched.

His breath was thick like smoke in the evening air, and despite the cold, he was breaking a sweat and had no need for a coat. After lifting the record player high above his head, he took a deep breath and then let out a scream so tormented that it sounded as if it came from someone else. The object was suspended above him. His arms trembled and the feeling of his muscles struggling to bear the weight brought a peculiar sense of relief. He took a step forward, screamed again and threw the record player onto the tarmac. Convinced that it would come apart and bits would fly into the air, Robbie jumped back but the bulky machine seemed to bounce off the road before settling, unhurt and upside down. His breathing was loud and laboured in the silence of the country. With a quickening pulse, he searched the hedge to find a stick large enough to do some damage.

Armed and dishevelled, he started to assault the player, all the while shouting as it sat solid and unflinching beneath him.

The stick eventually broke and Robbie let out a whimper of disbelief before hunkering down to inspect his work.

'I can't even break the bloody player,' he said, scoffing and wiping snot from his nose. 'Unbelievable.'

He gathered it in his arms again and, after identifying a large enough tree, took a few steps back to get a run at it. Not able to build up too much speed owing to the weight of the machine, he hurled it quite unconvincingly at the tree trunk, almost following it before securing his footing. His car's headlights did not illuminate that area and, as he scanned the undergrowth, the car radio picked up signal and the lyrics of a song made the hair stand up on the back of his neck. Unable to hear it clearly at first, he then identified it as 'Chirpy Chirpy Cheep Cheep' and immediately pictured the blonde woman from Middle of the Road in her electric blue flares. Humiliated, he ignored the music and searched the long grass until he found the player slightly scuffed but otherwise intact. He collapsed onto the verge to catch his breath and for several minutes leant against the tree trunk and listened to the song. 'Where's your mama gone? Far, far away.'

The music lasted only minutes before the signal was lost. The wet ground started to seep through his jeans and he felt foolish. How would his daughter react to him hurling a harmless record player at a tree trunk like a child? The thought of Amy in her baby grow and booties settled him. He could imagine her splashing around in the kitchen sink with legs that went into spasms of excitement and her fine hair slicked down by the water. Would she remember the times he used a plastic cup to pour water over her face until she laughed gleefully and made him forget himself? Or the nights that he would take her from Hannah and the two of them would climb the stairs slowly, he looking down into her tired face and she holding on to his thumb as if anchoring herself against the waves of sleep. He realised how much he wanted to see her as a toddler, awkward in her nappy and starting to talk; he needed to be sure that her transition from crèche to primary school was as seamless as it could be and that he could be there to answer her questions.

Robbie used the tree to push himself off the ground and he dusted the dirt from his trousers.

'I won't leave you, Amy,' he whispered. 'How could I ever leave you?'

The car took a while to start after the lights had drained the battery but soon Robbie was on the road with his resolve building and the resilient record player on the seat beside him.

Twenty-Six

On his journey back to Larkscroft, Robbie watched as the promise of the moon glowed on the horizon. He turned on the radio and sang along, drumming the beat on the steering wheel until the song ended and he flicked between stations to find something else. As the road dipped and he passed Montgomery's dairy farm, he realised that it was not the moon colouring the sky but the flames of a fire that wavered in a haze of black smoke. Robbie pressed his foot on the accelerator and his entire body lurched forward as he rounded the last corner and saw the roof of the farmhouse burning like tinder in a bonfire. After abandoning his car at the roadside, he ran past the neighbours who had gathered outside the gate. One of them called out that they had phoned the fire brigade but before Robbie knew what he was doing, he had burst through the shed doors into the farmyard to see if the hall window was unlatched.

It took him several minutes to work out that the fire was upstairs and entire sections of the roof had collapsed. It hissed and crackled above him, sending parts of the walls crashing onto the tarmac and causing a heat so fierce to accost him that he had to physically push against it. He used the handle of the outside broom to break the window and the glass shattered in symphony with the panes above him blowing out from the force of the fire. The smoke in the ground floor caused him to cough and he screamed for his father through the sleeve of his jacket. It was impossible to hear anything above the racket of the fire as the house creaked and fell apart. Robbie knelt on the carpet and crawled towards his father's room, calling his name as he went. The door was open but when he reached the bed he found it empty and started to panic.

'Dad,' he shouted. 'Where are you?'

He imagined that his father had fallen asleep in the living room in front of the television, or that he had tripped on the stairs where the fire was making a quick descent. Robbie struggled to think clearly enough to plan his next move. Where was Wendy? The moment he had the thought, he remembered the parent-teacher evening she had to go to and his promise that he would be back in time; he pictured the text message he had sent before going into Joan's: On my way, you head on. As he patted the floor around him in search of the bed, his hand struck a limb and he discovered his father collapsed on the ground in the corner.

'Dad, are you all right?'

There was no response and Robbie quickly removed his jacket and placed it over his father's face. Standing in the smoke was so difficult that Robbie's eyes started to water and he lost his bearings entirely. Light from the flames, which by now had travelled through the hallway to devour the doors of the living room, was illuminating the window that Robbie hoped to carry his father through but the heat held him back and he cried out in frustration.

With his father in his arms, he took a moment to assess any other possible exits but ended up facing the hallway and the open window again. John's body was limp and no heavier than his thin, young bride had been when he had carried her over the threshold of their home. Robbie turned his back to the flames and moved as quickly as he could into the hallway. The heat felt like day-old sunburn.

Every breath he took was laced with smoke and he worried

that he might collapse before getting his father to safety. The air coming from the open window allowed him a moment's reprieve as he turned to lower his father through the broken glass on to the picnic table. A crash sounded behind him as the bookcase fell within inches of his leg and the flames spread out across the floor. Scrambling through the window was dream-like; his legs would not co-operate and his clothes got caught on jagged pieces of glass. He cried out as pain shot through his foot and he used all his strength to give the final push that landed him in the yard. After lifting his father from the table, he managed to carry him only several steps before he was forced to lower him to the ground. In the background he could hear people shouting and what sounded like someone attempting to break the padlock on the yard gate.

In a fit of coughing that made his lungs ache, he collapsed beside his father and pressed his neck to find a pulse. His hands were shaking too violently to determine if anything was beating beneath his fingertips and the best he could do was gather his father into his lap and rock him. The house blazed in front of them, far enough away not to hurt them but close enough that they could feel its heat. A siren sounded in the distance and a sudden calm came over Robbie as he wiped the soot from his father's face and watched as the farmhouse groaned before giving in to the flames and collapsing. Sparks rose against the night sky as bits and pieces of the house fell like meteorites onto the tarmac.

'Son?'

Robbie looked down as his father wheezed beneath him.

'Dad,' he said, unbuttoning the top buttons of his pyjama top, 'just relax, an ambulance will be here soon.'

John turned in the direction of the house and closed his eyes tightly.

'It's ok, it's going to be ok,' Robbie said, stroking his hair.

He tried to speak but his voice was hoarse. Robbie could hear someone struggling with the bolt on the cattle gate.

'They'll be here soon.'

A male voice swore as he wrestled with the hawthorn tree and started to pull the gate open. His yellow Wellington boot kicked through the branches and he called for help.

'Where . . .?' Robbie heard his father whisper.

'Try not to speak, Dad.'

John started to wriggle and cough.

'Easy, easy,' Robbie said. He could tell that his father was intent on telling him something and he tried to support his back so that he was in a sitting position.

'Where . . . were . . . you?'

The firemen were through and as some of them pulled a length of hosepipe down the yard towards the house, two made their way towards Robbie and his father.

'I rescued you,' Robbie said, craning his neck to see his father better. As his forehead creased with confusion, he felt a sharp pain above his eye and realised that he must be injured.

'You left me alone.'

Robbie recoiled, not even registering the firemen's presence as they extracted his father from his arms. A fireman with smoke-stained cheeks and a hard hat knelt beside Robbie as his father was taken away.

'This one's in shock,' the fireman said without turning away from Robbie. 'You'll be all right, mate. You're safe now.'

ജ

'Do you ever get the feeling that life is like one of those spinning tops that has been going along just fine and then suddenly it starts to feel a bit wobbly and soon it's careening out of control?' Robbie said.

Elizabeth laid her hand on his arm.

'Come on, let's have a look at the damage.'

Wendy pulled into the driveway behind them. Robbie

watched her closely as she made straight for him and he lowered his head in anticipation of a scolding. When he felt her arms around him and the coldness of her nose on his neck, it took a few seconds for him to reciprocate the embrace. He held her while she soaked the collar of his jacket and squeezed him so tightly that his smoke-induced cough returned and forced them apart.

She stepped back, wiped her face roughly with the sleeve of her coat and turned to take in the sight of the farmhouse. Its charred remains still dripped from the firemen's soaking and the wind blew the bitter scent of smoke across the driveway. A door slammed shut behind them and, as Wendy walked over to speak to their neighbour, Robbie and Elizabeth picked their way across the front field to the cattle gate.

'This is where the firemen got through,' he said.

The gate was still ajar and Elizabeth set her small shoe into the footprint of a fireman's Wellingtons. A thick grey mist of cloud hung above them and made the scene in the yard more desolate and dreary than it had been the previous night.

'I broke this window with the broom; it's lower to the ground than the rest,' he explained.

His sister nodded and pulled at the remaining shards of glass in the frame.

'Let's go in through the kitchen,' he said.

Built on to the farmhouse by Robbie's grandfather, the kitchen stuck out from the rest of the house and had suffered no damage from the fire. Inside, it was possible to imagine that nothing was different but as soon as Elizabeth opened the door into the living room, they could see through to the hall where the fire had been snuffed out. Apart from some charring on the doorframes, the living room had suffered only smoke damage. The walls were sooty and the furniture soiled but when Elizabeth ran a wet finger over the table, the wood beneath came up clean. The hallway carpet crunched like snow beneath their feet as Elizabeth and Robbie made their way to the stairs.

'We'd better not go up there,' Robbie said, peering up the banister to the entrails of the roof.

Elizabeth ignored him and climbed the stairs, careful with her footing as if the whole thing might collapse beneath her at any moment. Robbie heard Wendy shouting from the yard and looked between Elizabeth's back and the kitchen.

'We're in here,' he shouted. 'Lizzie's going upstairs.'

Wendy appeared beside him and shouted at their younger sister to come down.

'Relax,' she shouted back. 'The floor will hold fine. I just want to have a look. Don't be such scaredy-cats.'

Robbie and Wendy looked at one another, shrugged and followed their sister. From the top of the stairs they could see that the roof had caved in over their father's old bedroom. A crow circled above the house and Robbie felt a shiver run the length of his spine. The walls had disintegrated to piles of what looked like charcoal, and the contents of Narnia were reduced to ashes.

'Look, Robbie,' Elizabeth said, pointing to the blackened corpse of the rocking horse in the corner. It had been protected by a large brass fireguard that had belonged to a distant relative and was too grand to look comfortable in the living room. Robbie grabbed the horse by its ears and pulled it to safety.

'That's about the only thing that's salvageable,' Wendy said.

'All those memories,' Elizabeth said, shaking her head, 'gone just like that. Mum's old wedding dress was in there somewhere and all our old school records and that grandfather clock you wanted to restore.'

'Oh well,' Wendy said. The wind from the broken window toyed with her hair. 'If there hadn't been so much food for the fire in here, perhaps Dad wouldn't have fared so well.'

The three were silenced.

'It's not as bad as I thought it was going to be,' Robbie said, stepping onto the landing to check the damage to his old bed-room. 'I thought the whole place would be razed to the ground.'

'You made it just in time,' Wendy said, her tone soft.

The door had been closed to his room and, although it looked as though the fire had travelled beneath the door to the carpet, the worst of the damage had been done by the water sprayed through the broken window.

'We'd better get going,' Wendy said, checking her watch. 'Dad will be wondering where we are.'

Robbie hung back as Elizabeth made her way down the stairs.

'Hey,' Wendy said, pointing her finger into his chest. 'This is not your fault, all right?'

The look in her eyes was fierce.

'Do you hear me?' she said.

He nodded but struggled to meet her eye.

'Do you?'

There was soot smeared across her right cheek that a tear had cut a path though.

'Yes, Wendy, I hear you.'

She nodded resolutely and repeated that it was time to go, before following Elizabeth downstairs.

Twenty-Seven

Two days later John was due to be discharged and it was decided between the siblings that they would approach their mother and ask if he might stay in her guest room. It was not an easy decision to make, with Robbie exploring every possible option in order to avoid his parents being under the same roof. Elizabeth had suggested he stay with Wendy, leading to a full disclosure of her home situation that made it clear why that would be impossible. Elizabeth bemoaned her choice of a one-bedroom apartment on the fifth floor, saying she would have taken him in had it not been for the cramped conditions and single bed. There had been several minutes of silence as the three drank the dregs of their coffee at the café opposite the hospital. Robbie had moved back into Margaret's house and his bedroom was next door to a second spare room used as a dumping ground for exercise equipment, paper work and the vacuum cleaner.

'If I cleared all that stuff out, Dad would have plenty of space and a decent view of the front garden,' Robbie said.

'There's no denying that the room would be perfect,' Wendy said. 'It's the fact that the room happens to be in our mother's house.'

'I know,' said Robbie. 'It's far from ideal but there are no other options.'

Elizabeth had laughed. 'This will be fun.'

They travelled together to their mother's house, leaving

themselves little time for a back-up plan if she refused.

'The farmhouse is wrecked,' Elizabeth told Margaret when their coats had been shed.

'I know, we drove past it this morning. I'm so glad you're all right.' She reached for Robbie's hand.

'It must have been the electrics. It's common enough in houses as old as the farmhouse,' Adam said.

'It's incredible how fast an entire house can be reduced to nothing,' Robbie said, taking a piece of shortbread from the plate his mother passed around. 'It just shows you.'

'Shows what?' Wendy asked.

'Not to hold too tightly to things.'

'A house isn't just things though, is it? I know the house was going to be torn down anyway but I wasn't ready for it to happen so soon,' Wendy said.

A contemplative silence fell in the room as pieces of sugary shortbread were dipped into tea and the family looked kindly at one another.

'What next?' Margaret asked.

Robbie and Wendy exchanged looks.

'I don't think I want to hear this,' Margaret said before Robbie had a chance to speak.

'He has nowhere to go, Mum.'

'Absolutely not.'

'Just hear us out.'

'I don't believe you're even going to ask me this.'

'What?' Adam asked.

'Mum,' Elizabeth started, 'you know we wouldn't ask unless we were desperate. There is literally no other option, and, well, it won't be for long.'

Robbie looked at his mother as if knowing that Elizabeth had trumped any possible argument she might have. Margaret's lips moved but no words came out. She looked with panic from one child to the next before dropping her head onto her chest and sighing. Adam put his arm around her shoulders.

'We'll do it,' he said, squeezing Margaret as he spoke. She turned her head towards him.

'We will? No offence, Adam, but you don't really know what you're getting yourself in to.'

'He is a dying man, Maggie. It's the least we can do.'

Margaret groaned.

'Well, since you're all ganging up on me . . .'

'You'll take him?' Elizabeth said, raising her eyebrows.

'All right, all right. But you can clear all the junk out of there,' she said to Adam, pointing in the direction of the spare room. 'And don't expect me to do anything for him. You kids are responsible for his care, do you hear me?'

The three nodded and Robbie checked the time.

'We'd better go. Lizzie, why don't you stay and work on the room. Wendy and I can go to the hospital.'

'One more thing,' Margaret said as Robbie took his coat from the stand. 'I want to be there when he, you know . . .'

Robbie waited for her to complete the sentence.

'Dies?' Wendy asked.

'Well, yes.'

'Why?' Wendy pressed.

'I don't have to explain myself, Wendy, it's just one of the conditions.'

'Fine,' Robbie said, lifting his car keys from the sideboard.

∞

When the ambulance pulled into the driveway, Robbie skirted around the paramedics, feeling obsolete. Margaret and Adam had not returned from their lunch date and Robbie was glad to be spared an awkward hallway conversation between his parents. He wondered whether his mother, if given the chance, would gloat over John being so reduced that he was forced to take refuge in her house.

Robbie knew when his father passed no remark on his accommodation that his illness had accelerated. The room had been transformed into a bright, airy space, and owing to its position on the corner of the house, it got both the morning and afternoon sun. It smelt of disinfectant but the bed was ready and Elizabeth had set up her television in the corner. With the jingle for *Countdown* playing in the background, Elizabeth and Wendy fussed around their father until he eyeballed them to leave him be. His face against the crisp, white pillowcase was yellowing and gaunt. He looked from the commode in the corner that the occupational therapist had left, to the bowl of watermelon segments on the table before motioning for Wendy not to stand between him and the television.

Robbie spent the following days curled in the armchair in his father's room. Since the morphine patches had gone on, none of them had been able to communicate with their father and they had to content themselves with the silence and occasional visits from the district nurse.

The skin on John's face had lost all elasticity and was draped around his ears and neck as though the effort of keeping it taut across his cheeks was too great. His mouth was always open and his lips were dry and cracked from the heat of the room. Stale breath was exhaled in a slow, unsteady rhythm and occasionally he would cough and wake himself up.

Wendy had said 'good' when Robbie told her he had been to see Joan. She did not ask any more about the content of their conversation. Lizzie, on the other hand, was inquisitive enough to make him wish he had not told her. 'What did you say?' 'What did she say?' 'How did you feel?' 'How was it left?' 'What happens next?'

His younger sister had a remarkable interest in the details of a story and while part of him felt privileged to be the object of such intense questioning, he was not sure how much he wanted to give away. The telling of a thing often reduced it before it had chance to become a fully formed thought.

'When I get things straight in here,' he said, tapping his head, 'you'll be the first to know.'

'Ok, but I might be dead by then.' He moved to slap her on the arm and she dodged out of his way. She had brought a tub of Vaseline into the room and Robbie watched while she spread it gently on their father's lips. She hummed gently and Robbie looked away.

&c

A week later Elizabeth came into the kitchen while Wendy and her mother were stewing plums to put into their porridge, and Robbie was reading the newspaper. The district nurse had been in that morning and Elizabeth had stayed in the room for his prognosis. Her face was drawn and her eyes worried. Robbie watched his mother look down at her nightdress as if it were unsuitable for what was about to happen.

'What?' she said.

'The nurse has suggested a vigil,' Elizabeth said, biting the inside of her cheek and looking back towards their father's room. 'I don't want to miss it.'

'It's not an eclipse, Elizabeth, or, or, some movie star we want to get a look at,' Wendy jumped in.

No one spoke.

'Oh God, I'm sorry.' Wendy grabbed the countertop with both hands and rocked. Elizabeth and Robbie both stood beside her, cautious to lay a hand on her shoulder. She turned and reached out an arm to each of them so the three stood entwined in the middle of the kitchen. Robbie could see that his mother was trying to steady herself with the back of a chair. One hand was against her ribcage, bracing herself as if out of breath after physical exercise. She watched her children with what looked to Robbie like envy and yet something held her back from going to them. Her insecurity was difficult to watch and Robbie was glad to see her stand up straight when the three of them disengaged. Wendy turned off the stove.

'I'm not really hungry any more,' she said, putting the lid on the porridge.

Their father had his eyes closed when they went into the room but opened them when Elizabeth turned down the volume on the television. Robbie thought it would have been strange to watch his father die with *Ready Steady Cook* in the background but the silence was as difficult to bear. He excused himself to get the record player out of his car boot and carried it into the house. The scuffs had been cleaned and a new needle attached. When Wendy saw the player, she smiled and Robbie was grateful for her kindness. Margaret, who was hanging back from the bedside, took the opportunity to be useful and selected a record.

'Some Klughardt for you,' she whispered as the needle settled and the haunting music of the viola sounded.

'It's a bit depressing,' Elizabeth said. She had taken their father's hand and was stroking the veins that stood out on his skin.

'At the beginning it is,' Wendy agreed.

'Do you remember the story?' Margaret said, sitting on the chair that Robbie had pulled out for her. Wendy nodded, Elizabeth shook her head and Robbie was sure that he saw his father's eyelids flutter.

'A poet called Nikolaus Lenau was born to German parents in Hungary in eighteen hundred and something. Even as a young boy, he was unhappy with his situation in life and he started travelling all over Hungary and Germany trying to make peace with himself. He was influenced by a lot of the romantic poets of that time who wrestled with melancholy and the idea that happiness and hope were always just out of reach. He set sail for America, believing that he would find what he was looking for there. But once again his search for peace was unsuccessful and his poetry is full of the disappointment that he experienced as a result.'

She paused as the oboe rose above the cello and then wrapped itself like a ribbon around the lower string song.

'Back in Hungary following a disastrous romance, Nikolaus spent his days wandering along the Danube writing poetry. The reeds along the banks of the river, coupled with his grief at being alone and out of love, led to him writing *Schilflieder*, or Reed Songs as it has been translated. The five verses chart the emotions of the poet in the wake of his failed relationship. Klughardt found the poetry so beautiful that he put music to it. This is the piece he composed and each movement tries to capture the grief, loneliness and nostalgia of the poem.'

There were tears in her voice as she finished and the music played on for several seconds before running out and leaving only the sound of static.

'His breathing seems to be getting slower,' Elizabeth said.

The four stood and pressed in closer to the bedside. Although the moment was inevitable and had been building like thunder for weeks, suddenly it was impossible for Robbie to believe that this was his father's life reaching its conclusion. The last words he had spoken were to berate Robbie for his absence when the house went up in flames and now he was not lucid enough to offer closure to any of his family members.

As he tried to fight panic, he realised that he had been holding out for a resolution or a brief exchange where they might exonerate one another. The scratching of the record and John's rasping provided an eerie backdrop for his death but as the minutes stretched on, the family took their seats again and looked wearily at one another.

The time between each breath seemed to stretch interminably until one of them would be convinced that it was definitely his last. Just as they got to their feet his chest would rise and his breath would be drawn out, as though something was caught in his throat and was struggling to break free. By the time the nurse arrived at lunchtime, the family was exhausted and, after assuring them that she would call if there was any change, Robbie, his sisters and Margaret made themselves lunch.

'Do you want a sandwich?' Margaret offered the nurse when she had finished her visit.

'I'm all right, thanks.'

'How is he?' Elizabeth asked.

'He's done well to hang on this long. I didn't expect him to still be here, to be honest with you. He's a real fighter.'

'Indeed,' Margaret said, clearing the lunch plates.

'He has lost consciousness which means that he probably won't hold on for much longer.'

'This waiting is driving me mad,' Wendy said, laughing as if to take the edge off.

'I know,' the nurse said. 'This is the hardest part. Just keep talking to him. The hearing is the last to go, you know?'

'Really?' Margaret said. 'We've been playing him music. Will he have heard it?'

'Chances are he did,' she said and Margaret slipped out to put the record back on.

After a few minutes, Robbie saw the nurse to the door and made his way back into the bedroom. He could tell immediately that his father was gone. The injustice of missing his passing was like being punched. He felt it as the final rejection from his father, who had no intention of allowing him to make sense of his past. Margaret looked over and held his stare. She stood, somewhat awkwardly, with a daughter on each arm but as he moved forward, Elizabeth stepped out of her mother's embrace and took hold of his arm.

'We've all said goodbye,' she said, motioning for him to do the same.

His father's withered body seemed so far removed from the tyrant of his youth. Gone were the ruddy cheeks that flared after one too many drinks and burned late in to the night. Gone too was the sturdy frame that made him an imposing presence in a room and put muscle behind his tantrums. There was so little left of him that was recognisable and now there would be no opportunity to fight back or demand answers.

'Dad . . .' he began.

John's lips were turned down at their edges as if in disapproval. Robbie felt Elizabeth tighten her grip.

'You were a bastard,' he said, laughing gently. 'You were a bastard and we were all scared of you . . .'

He heard one of his sisters sniff and a door close somewhere in the house. Unsure of the reaction to his admission, he kept his head down and studied his father's fingernails. They were discoloured and splitting, with none of the soil beneath them that was characteristic of his hands. These were the hands that had lifted him as a baby and steadied him as a toddler. They would have shown tenderness to Margaret and been used to build things, grow vegetables and calm animals. Their purpose could not be reduced to a tight fist or a white knuckle around a whiskey bottle. From the other side of the bed his mother's voice came quietly.

'You were a terrible husband, John.'

Robbie met her eye. Her cheeks were sodden and some of her hair was plastered to her face. She was holding a tissue over her mouth as if to prevent herself from saying any more. Elizabeth was rigid beside him and Wendy did not seem to be bothered by the accusations that she spent so much of her life rebuffing.

'You really . . .' Wendy started. Robbie watched her fighting with herself, wrestling with the reality of their father's underwhelming death. 'You really made my life difficult, Dad.'

Until that moment Robbie had been dry-eyed but his older sister laying bare her pain was difficult to hear. Refusing to take a tissue from the box at the bedside, Robbie blinked furiously and looked at the ceiling. After several minutes of silence, Elizabeth leaned over their father's corpse and touched his face. Her hands covered his forehead, his cheeks and down to his neck, stroking it gently as if memorising his skin.

'I don't even know you,' she said, leaning in closer. 'You were never there.' She removed her hand and shrugged.

Margaret sat down and looked from one child to the other. Sunk low in the chair, she seemed defeated and Robbie might have hugged her had Wendy not got there first.

'You'd better call the doctor,' their mother said to no one in particular. 'Why don't you put the kettle on and I'll be in shortly.'

The three siblings left the room as Margaret pulled her chair closer to the bed.

Twenty-Eight

Despite Robbie's fears that his father's hermitic lifestyle would have cut his friends off for good, his mother's house was full on the evening of his passing. Sandwiches had to be ordered from the pub: egg and scallion, ham and mustard and tuna fish mashed with mayonnaise. They arrived on silver trays, cut into bite-sized triangles and smothered with cellophane wrap. Margaret had made several plates of iced cupcakes, a homemade quiche and shortbread. Her cheeks were flushed and her eyes wild. Adam hovered beside her.

Robbie had no time to speak to her as the living room filled with people and the windows steamed from their body heat. It was raining so heavily that those running from their cars to the front door were soaked through to their under layers. Umbrellas and raincoats littered the hallway and hung on the banisters, the water soaking the carpet so that visitors left wet footprints all over his mother's good front room.

It reminded Robbie of going to church as a child. It was a cramped, damp building with windows that did not keep out the wind and walls that were wet to the touch. At the beginning of the service people would huddle together in the pews, to save space and generate heat but by the end women were fanning themselves with hymn books and the air was musty. Forbidden to unbutton his shirt or remove his hat, Robbie would feel the sweat trickle from his forehead down to his collar and fight the claustrophobia of his aunt's knees squashing him into his mother.

It was the same sense of claustrophobia that sent him in and out of the kitchen to ply the guests with snacks that evening. Forced to wriggle his way between Dromore's oldest and queerest, he would appear at an elbow offering sausage rolls and then excuse himself by saying that there were too many mouths to feed for him to dilly-dally. In truth, the pressure of having to explain his absence for the past five years was awkward. He did not want to set the tray down, take a break or have a conversation.

'Robbie,' a familiar voice called behind him. He turned to see Joe Toppley standing with two other men he did not recognise. They were in the hallway between the living room and the room in which his father had died. It was cooler there and Robbie set his tray on the large windowsill beside them.

'Joe,' he said, reaching out his hand. 'Good to see you.' Joe pretended to be offended by the hand and reached over to hug him. Robbie felt him squeeze his shoulders and the kindness in his affection caused a lump to grow in his throat. He pulled away and tried to laugh.

'I'm sorry for your loss,' the man standing to the right of Joe said.

'Thank you.'

'This here is one of your father's oldest acquaintances,' Joe said by way of introduction. 'The pair of them went around together in school and even dabbled in a bit of business. Am I right, Patrick?'

'Aye, you're right, Joe.' His face was covered in large brown moles, some of which were sprouting whiskers. He regarded Robbie with interest and his lips wobbled when he spoke.

'Your father was a cunning businessman, did you know that?'

'No, I didn't.'

'He started selling comic books and sweets in school and by

the time I knew him, it was second-hand cars and just about anything a man wanted. He was only sixteen then.'

'Really?'

'Oh yes,' he said, seeing that Robbie was sceptical. 'He only went into farming when your grandfather died and in all the years Larkscroft Farm was in your family's hands, your father was the first to turn a decent profit.'

Joe and the other man nodded.

'Back in the day it was quite a farm,' the other man chipped in. 'Men came from all over the county to buy everything from tomatoes to manure. On a Saturday it was like a marketplace, with tables set up all over that front field full of whatever was in season. And your da, he never rested. No, he was always at something, wasn't he Joe?'

Joe nodded.

'Aye, if he wasn't growing grapevines in the greenhouses, he was curing his own hams in the laundry room or burning up wood to sell as charcoal in the summer. He was always scheming.'

The men laughed and shook their heads. Robbie looked at his shoes.

'That doesn't sound much like my father, I have to be honest with you.'

Joe patted his shoulder.

'No, Robbie. Things had changed a bit by the time you came along.'

'The drink does a terrible thing to a man. It turns him inside out, takes all the love and passion he had for lots of different things and channels it into a single obsession. I've seen it manys a time in my life,' the man with the moles said, shaking his head and speaking more to himself than to any of them.

Robbie picked up the tray of sandwiches and noticed that some of them had split open to reveal buttered pieces of ham. Joe held him by the elbow and Robbie saw that he had tears in his eyes, the kind of tears that old men give themselves over to quite freely.

'It may be difficult for you to believe, Robbie, but your father was an excellent sort of man and we were all the better for knowing him.'

The other two men echoed their agreement as Robbie smiled, thanked them and ducked into the kitchen.

'Do you get the feeling that we're at someone else's wake?' Elizabeth whispered to him. The room was full of women bustling to and fro with knives to cut cake and tea towels to dry dishes. Their mother was nowhere to be seen.

'I mean,' Elizabeth continued. 'I've never even met half of these people and they seem to be talking about a man I don't know.'

'Yep,' Robbie said, loading his tray with more sandwiches.

'Did you know that Dad won medals for show-jumping?'

'What?' Robbie said, his mouth full of a cheese and pickle sandwich.

'See that little huddle of people in the corner by the TV? Her with the blue rinse and the man wearing what looks like velvet, but is actually some sort of imitation suede?'

Robbie laughed.

'Well they used to ride with Dad. They said he was one of the best.'

They were interrupted by a tall, thin woman with high cheekbones and pursed, pink lips. Robbie felt dizzy from looking at the brightly coloured, patterned blouse she was wearing that floated about her torso when she moved.

'I remember you when you were squatting on a potty in the kitchen,' she said to Elizabeth. Robbie almost choked on the last mouthful of his sandwich.

'Lovely,' Elizabeth said.

'You had the fattest little knees. I used to tell your mother to stop feeding you or else you'd burst.' She threw her head back and cackled so loudly that the huddle of women beside them looked over. Robbie sneaked a glance at his sister, who was trying to laugh along.

'Helen,' she said, extending her hand to Elizabeth.

'Elizabeth, and my brother Robbie.'

'No!' she said, refusing to relinquish Robbie's hand. 'Your mother never said.'

'Said what?'

'That the prodigal had returned.'

Robbie squirmed and she allowed him to extract his hand.

'Mind you, I haven't seen your mother in what feels like a hundred years, so what do I know? Where is she anyway?' She looked over her shoulder, the skin around her eyes pinched in concentration. 'Never mind, I'm sure we'll bump into one another sooner or later. What I really wanted to say was that I'm sorry for your loss, not that I'm terribly upset that your father is no longer with us, but your father is your father, am I right?'

Elizabeth's mouth was agape. Robbie agreed, hoping she would move on.

'I heard about the fire,' she said. 'Must have been terrible for you but it makes things easier in the long run, doesn't it?'

'Excuse me?' Elizabeth said, her shoulders square.

'I'm Helen, Helen Spiers, wife of James Spiers, owner of the land that your shell of a farmhouse is on. Don't just take my word for it, there's a great big sign in the front garden,' she said, laughing. 'Naturally we allowed your poor father to stay on there, knowing he was getting on in years. To be honest with you, it hasn't been a great time to build anyway, what with the economy in a bit of a mess.' She said it like it was a secret. Robbie moved closer to his sister.

'But you can never be sure what's round the corner, that's what James always says. And that's a prime piece of land. Despite what everyone has been saying, and I know there's been a lot of talk, James won't lose out on this property, mark my words. He may have paid a hefty price for it – your father always had a good business head - but it'll sell for a whole lot more when my James is finished with it. Have you seen the plans?'

Robbie shook his head, Elizabeth was mute beside him.

'We'll tear down what's left of the house – that's the first step and the fire gave us a head start – and we'll get rid of those outbuildings that are such a hazard. I'm amazed your father wasn't killed knocking about in them. The whole place will be flattened and levelled out, and then we'll build eight very tasteful bungalows and a small block of apartments. You won't know the place. And let me tell you—'

'Let me tell you something, Mrs. Spiers—'

'Lizzie,' Robbie said, taking her arm.

'No, Robbie, I won't be spoken to like this with my father not even cold.' She turned to the woman who was smoothing her blouse and looking around her.

'Unless you hadn't realised, the other guests are here to pay their respects to my dead father. I'm not too sure why you're here but I consider it very rude of you to talk about knocking the house down that my father lived in his whole life.'

'Well—'

Elizabeth leaned in closer.

'That house has been in my family for generations and I'd thank you to have a little bit of respect.'

Robbie watched as his sister turned away but then, reconsidering, turned back to the woman and asked her to leave.

'Excuse me?' Helen said, looking at the women around her who had, by this time, taken a keen interest in the conversation. 'I know you must be grieving, my dear, but this is quite unnecessary.'

'You are not welcome here and I'm asking you to leave.'

Helen laughed, pressed her lips together and made her way to the front door. It was then that Robbie caught a glimpse of his mother through the kitchen window. Noting that Elizabeth had been absorbed by a circle of clucking women, he found his coat and crept into the backyard.

The rain had eased and the clouds were parted over the house to reveal the moon, full and dimpled like a golf ball. The trees in the garden were weather-beaten and forlorn and his mother's wind chime tinkled on the decking. He squelched his way across the mossy path to the river and found her with knees tucked into her chest beneath a sycamore.

'It's been a long time since you've needed to hide out beneath a tree,' Robbie said, ducking beneath the branches and dusting the ground beside her before sitting down.

'I knew you'd come,' she said, putting a hand on his knee. 'You were the only one who ever came.'

'I was the only one who knew where to find you, Mum.'

'Or the only one who looked.'

'Oh come on, don't get all philosophical.'

She let out a deep sigh.

'I just didn't want to be in there.'

'I know.'

'It's not my place. I feel awkward.'

Robbie took her hand.

'The place you are now is a much happier one.'

'Do you think so?'

'Sure it is.'

'I didn't know what you'd make of us. Of me, of Adam. I'm a different person from the mother you left behind; at least I feel very different. And Adam . . . well, he's just Adam.'

They both laughed.

'He sure is.'

The image of his mother in her wedding dress standing next to his father came back to him again and he could picture the youth in her skin and the fear in her eyes.

'Mum?'

'Yes.'

'What was it like for you, you know, in the beginning with Dad.'

'It's funny, Robbie. Maybe it's seeing some of his old friends again or just the kindness that comes when someone dies but I've been remembering those days so clearly and fondly this week.'

She looked away.

'He was a different man, the kind of man I spent the best part of my marriage hoping he'd turn back into. There was a determination in him to be the best at whatever he did, and nine times out of ten he succeeded. He was courageous in his risk-taking and most of the time it paid off; he was serious about his commitments and as honest and kind a man as you'd find. Not one to talk much, that was for certain, but very gentle and patient. I was the luckiest girl in the town when he asked me to marry him and that's the truth.'

His mother's eyes above the lace trimmings of her wedding dress had haunted Robbie for weeks. It was the same look that he saw so often as a young boy, a look that said, 'Don't tell me the worst because I know it already'. It was fear and cowardice and it meant that she never had the power to change the things that needed changing.

'Did you ever see anything in him that might have warned you . . .'

She was quiet for a long time, so long that Robbie thought she might not have heard him.

'One day I watched him play football for our local club. He was one of the best players on the team and, because of that, all the girls loved him. The match was in Newry and there was a lot riding on Dromore's success. It was a wet and windy day but so many people had turned out that there weren't enough seats and we had to stand throughout the game. I didn't mind though; someone had hot coffee and your father's friends held large black umbrellas over my head. The match was so exciting and I remember feeling happy to be a part of something. We weren't engaged at that point but I knew it was coming and had no reservations about saying yes.'

She paused and started to rub her hands on her trousers.

'The score was even with only a few minutes to go until full-time. I don't understand much about football but a player from the Newry side fouled someone in the Dromore team and we got a penalty. Well, the fans went crazy because it meant that your father, the top goal scorer in the team, had to take the shot.'

She sighed.

'He never missed a shot, like most things in his life, and was full of confidence as he prepared to kick the ball. It was such an easy angle that people in the crowd were already celebrating Dromore's win but somehow your father missed it and the fans were stunned. I could see that he was confused. He kept looking at his foot, then the ball, then the goal, but there were still a few minutes left of play and he had to move. Newry took advantage of the team's shock and scored a goal with one minute to go.'

She let out a long breath and when she spoke again her voice was unsteady.

'Your father was supposed to take me home that night but I waited around in the cold outside the changing room for so long that eventually someone else offered. I didn't hear from him for two weeks after that but rumours around town were that he had been in Dempsey's for seven solid days. When he finally reappeared, he seemed to be in flying form. He denied everything about Dempsey's, said he had been sick and whisked me off to Portstewart for the day. Perhaps it sounds foolish now, and it's not too big a deal to lose a football match and drown your sorrows, but it was the excess. I suppose you'd call it bingeing now.'

Robbie leaned his head against the tree trunk, trying to imagine his father as a high achiever, a soccer player, a business-man. The multiple identities of the man he was before he started drinking gave him such a deep sadness that he was not sure he could stand up under the weight.

He could feel the question burning on his tongue, wanting to be asked and settled, although its truth he already knew. Would it make him feel better hearing his mother say it? Could it make her strong, help him heal, allow them to let go? The wind picked up and he could feel her shifting beside him, wanting to leave.

'Before we go, Mum, I have to know. What changed him?'

The question, once asked, made him uncomfortable. There was too much of himself in it and left little to hide behind when his mother turned on him, her eyes so full of pity that he felt embarrassed.

'That was the thing,' she said, diverting her gaze. 'It was the fear of failing that crippled him. In our first few years, things were good. I was his business partner, his wife and his friend. We laughed a lot, went most places together and tended to our garden with an awareness of our responsibility for our crops that was almost holy. But when I fell pregnant with Wendy, the initial joy he expressed gave way to a fear such as I have never known. I thought I'd be the frightened one; I've been scared of things all my life. But I wasn't. This person was growing inside me and it felt like the most natural thing in the world. Your father, on the other hand, just slipped away.

'It was slow at first. He'd stay out a night or two during the week, full of believable excuses and minty breath when he returned. Things were tougher for a farmer then. Supermarkets were springing up everywhere with lower prices than we could afford to compete with. Your father had to grow cash crops instead of the things he loved so much to experiment with.'

'I remember the cabbages,' Robbie said, stalling the story.

'Yes, those were a bit further down the line. He started with potatoes, but they took up so much space in the garden and he wasn't prepared to cut down the fruit trees; when he had the chance to rent the field next door, someone told him there was money in roses.'

'Roses?'

'Oh, Robbie, it was beautiful. I was full term with you when they bloomed; an entire field full of every colour of rose that you can imagine. They day you were born, your father came to the hospital with the biggest bunch of apricot-coloured roses I had ever seen.'

'Why didn't he keep that up?'

'It didn't make anywhere near what your father was expecting. Some of the buyers fell through, they lost their value, something along those lines. I was otherwise occupied at that time with a toddler and a new baby. The pressure of two tiny children at the end of a long and fruitless day was just too much for him.'

'That must have been so hard for you, Mum.'

Although it was dark, Robbie could feel her eyes on him.

'Yes, Robbie, yes it was.'

He could imagine his young mother suckling him while trying to keep tabs on Wendy. Perhaps the bunch of roses was in a vase on top of the fireplace and she looked up at it from the sofa, watching the clock, not knowing when her husband would be home. His first memories as a child mostly excluded his father. There were one or two vague instances where he accompanied them to a park beside the sea and lifted Robbie up to reach the monkey bars but mostly he remembered his mother, tired, impatient and alone.

They sat in silence for several minutes.

'There's something else you should know.'

Robbie swallowed. 'What?'

'Your father, he . . .'

The river purled below them and looked glassy in the dark.

'It was a long time ago,' she said, turning her face away.

'What is it, Mum?'

'Oh, Robbie. I have been debating whether or not I should

tell you this for weeks. I even went to see your father, would you believe? It would have been better coming from him.'

'What would? Just tell me, you're making me nervous.'

'When you were living up in Belfast, your father spent his Friday nights in Boyles and I had the shame of driving down at one o'clock in the morning to pick him up. Normally I'd sit outside in the car and he'd stumble out at closing into the back seat. Then I got fed up and one night I went in there at midnight to find him. That was when people still smoked inside and I remember coughing my way round the tables. He had his back to me and the attention of every man in that corner of the bar was on him.'

She stopped and covered her mouth with her hand.

'Don't cry, Mum.'

After pushing his hand away, she took a deep breath and continued.

'He was talking about you, Robbie. He was telling everyone about your job, who you worked for, boasting about it to the whole pub. Elizabeth used to tell me things about your work and I told your father, thinking, stupidly, that it would help your relationship, or make him proud. He was proud that night, all right, but he gave everything away. He told them about Martin, about how the two of you were fighting for justice, I can't remember the specifics but it was too late by the time I got him to shut up.'

The sandwiches that Robbie had eaten began to churn in his stomach.

'Stupid fool didn't even remember what he'd said the next day. When I heard that Martin was shot that weekend, all I could think about was the faces of those men at the table, more sober than your father and smiling at me when I dragged him away. Victor Green was the worst, standing up to help me as though he was a decent sort of man—'

'Green?'

'Your Adrian's father. Victor.'

Robbie rolled forward on to his knees. His mind raced to fit the information into some sort of order that would make sense.

'I don't know what to say, son. I wanted him to tell you but it's my fault, I should never have told him anything.'

'Don't say that, this is not your fault. I just can't believe . . .'

A car started in the front driveway and Margaret looked towards the house.

'You'd better go in, Mum. The girls will be wondering where you are.'

'What about you?'

'I just need a minute.'

She stood but then hesitated in front of him before walking up the garden. Wake-goers talked and laughed in the kitchen that sent its light onto the decking. Robbie watched as she paused on the edge of the darkness. He turned his attention back to the river and took a pebble from the water that had been smoothed by the current. His heart was racing and he wished he had a cigarette to hand. The surface of the stone was damp to the touch. He wondered how things might have been different if his father had summoned the courage to make the admission. Throwing the pebble into the air, he caught it and slipped it into his pocket before turning his back on the river and going into the house.

Twenty-Nine

A thick mist had settled on the morning of the funeral. The sun was attempting to shine through it and making ghosts of commonplace things. Robbie stood at his bedroom window for several minutes, taking in the view of the river and the soggy fields beyond. Something stirred in the room and he turned to watch Hannah change her sleeping position and start to nuzzle the pillow. She and Amy had arrived the day before, two hours later than expected owing to the traffic coming out of Dublin.

Hannah had been flustered and felt like a stranger, while his daughter had grown at least two inches in his absence. The first ten minutes of their reunion was spent poking and prodding Amy until they had discussed all her features and had to shift their attention to one another. At that point his family had taken over and Hannah was swept into the frenzied emotion of his mother's house while Elizabeth stole Amy away to a quiet corner of the living room. Wendy and Margaret plied Hannah with tea and leftover tray bakes from the wake and when Robbie excused himself on 'funeral-related' business, she had looked up at him rosy-cheeked from the attention.

After visiting the florist to pay for their family wreath and some flowers for the church, Robbie had driven up the A1 to Hillsborough. The quaint shops and squashed houses with their neat window boxes reminded him of Ranelagh or Rathmines; suburbs that, at one stage, were villages on the outskirts of

Dublin before the great city loosened its belt and expanded.

With his hood pulled up against the rain and hands sunk deep into his pockets, he walked down the steep hill on Main Street. He saw smoke snaking from the chimney of The Plough and felt warmer at the sight of it. Inside, he ordered a cup of coffee and sat down in a small nook near the fire. He had only taken a few sips of his drink when Joan appeared, shaking the rain from her coat and signalling to the waiter that she too would like a coffee.

'Miserable day,' she said, rubbing her hands and then offering her palms to the fire. Catching his eye, she tugged on the edges of her blouse and sat down opposite him.

'I'm so sorry about, you know,' she said.

'Thanks.'

'When's the funeral?'

'This afternoon.'

'Martin's funeral was such a bollocks.'

'Was it?'

'Yes, the bishop was a new guy and he was very nervous. They couldn't do an open casket because, well, you know.'

Robbie nodded.

'Of course, Great-aunt Deirdre didn't know all the details about how he died and she was furious that the casket was closed. It was a whole palaver.' Her laugh came out more as a nervous titter.

He shifted in his seat.

'What?' Joan asked.

Robbie looked up.

'You just sighed as if the entire world was on your shoulders.'

'Sorry,' he said. 'I've just got a lot on my mind.'

'You look tired. Are you sleeping?'

'Not really.'

The waiter delivered Joan's coffee and she stirred sugar into it.

'I'm going home soon and there's something I need to tell you,' he said.

Joan sat upright and wrapped her hands around the mug.

'Go on then.'

'There is a possibility that it was all my fault. —Don't say anything yet. You know how close I was with Lizzie back then. Well, I told her stuff I shouldn't have and I have recently discovered that she told my mum, who told my dad, who blabbed to the whole pub by the sounds of things.'

He ate the foam on his cappuccino with a spoon. Joan was staring at him and he braced himself for her reaction.

'Listen, Robbie. It wasn't your fault. It wasn't anybody's fault. I've spent the last five years trying to find someone to blame. You were an easy target but I've been doing a lot of thinking these past few weeks and I just have to accept that Martin made choices that resulted in his own death.'

'But—'

'No, Robbie. It doesn't matter what your dad said or who he said it to. The end result was inevitable.'

He ran his fingers through his hair and watched her closely.

'It's not fair,' he said.

She laughed.

'Of course it's not fair.'

'That letter Martin wrote me. He wanted me to look after you and the girls.'

'Sure you were only young yourself.'

A dirty ring had formed on the inside of his coffee cup where the foam had started to thicken. He scraped at it with his teaspoon.

'Why are you being so nice?' he said.

'As I said, I've been doing a lot of thinking. I always imagined seeing you again and allowing all my rage out.' She flung her arms open. 'When you arrived at the house the other night, I realised that it wasn't right to blame you. I suppose it was just easier.'

'I'm sorry,' he said.

She took the coffee cup from him and wrapped her fingers around his.

'I know you are. That word is banned from now on, do you hear me?'

'Will you be ok?'

'Me? Of course.'

'Do you need to talk about . . .' he offered half-heartedly.

'No. I thought I did but really, there's not much more to say. You better get going.'

They exchanged a smile and Robbie checked his pockets for change.

'Bye, Joan,' he said, setting some coins on the table. 'Take care of yourself.'

ℨ

The mist had not lifted by the time the hearse arrived to collect the coffin. Two men in tall black hats handled the casket into the back of the car while Hannah packed Amy's things in a bag. Robbie tarried on the doorstep as the sleek, black vehicle reversed on to the road. There was something painfully final about watching his father's body leave and he wished it could have been from the farmhouse.

John had arrived on the doorstep of Larkscroft on the eve of his own father's death, only to have the keys thrust into his hand and an earnest plea made that he do a better job than his father. It was a story John loved to tell when he was trying to convert Robbie into a farmer. Even the memory of those conversations, some sober, others not, caused such a sense of responsibility to rise in Robbie that he wanted to uproot the billboard in the front field and lay claim to the land that should have been his. He laughed at himself and leant against the doorframe as the hearse drove slowly down the lane.

His melodrama gave way to a less severe kind of guilt when

he imagined how his father must have felt to know that Larkscroft Farm stopped with him. The sweat and blood that he had poured into the place out of respect for his own father and a need to support his family would soon be buried under new houses and fresh tarmac. What must it have felt like for him to sign it all over to someone like James Spiers? Robbie shivered as the car disappeared from sight and the mist started to soak through his clothes.

It fell on Robbie to give an address at the funeral. He had gone to Hillsborough Forest Park after his meeting with Joan to think about what he might say, but the words would not come. He could not think of anything that would be both true and appropriate to say in a church. How could he be expected to stand up and eulogise about a father who was always there but never present, had principles but no integrity, and whose death left more questions than answers. After enough laps of the lake that he lost count, Robbie phoned the minister to let him know that there would be no speech from a family member.

There was a deep silence in the church as the organ faded and the minister opened his bible on the podium.

'Do not let your hearts be troubled. You believe in God; believe also in me. My Father's house has many rooms; if that were not so, would I have told you that I am going there to prepare a place for you? And if I go and prepare a place for you, I will come back and take you to be with me that you also may be where I am. You know the way to the place where I am going.'

Robbie took Hannah's hand.

The casket was open at the front of the church with Robbie's family's wreath still covered in dew and white roses. When it was delivered to the house and set up in the room in which John had spent the last few days of his life, Robbie had been disarmed by his father's expressionless face. With smooth cheeks and less of a ruddy complexion, Robbie wanted to reach out and touch him but could not quite believe that his father would not open his eyes and scowl at him for trying. With John neck-deep in floral bouquets, Robbie allowed some of the relief from his death to settle.

The minister finished and the organ started up again, the notes running into one another as if they were racing to the end of the bar. Robbie stood between Hannah and Elizabeth. His daughter was asleep in her car seat with her hands clasped as if in prayer. Robbie took his wife's hand and whispered in her ear, 'I'm so glad I'm coming home with you'.

She was still looking at him as he took up the hymnbook to join in the singing.

Epilogue

It had not snowed at Christmas since Robbie was a teenager. It had been forecast on the weather report as they drove up from Dublin the previous day and when Adam phoned that morning he had seen the bright, white light coming through the curtains and threw them open for Hannah. They sat for several minutes looking out over Wendy's garden, which had been buried up to its neck in the overnight blizzard. A few starlings disturbed the snow on the branches of a willow tree and plastic toys belonging to Robbie's nephews looked like items of clothing creating lumps under a duvet. He left Hannah at his sister's house with directions to the church, just as Amy and his nephews were waking up.

Half an hour later, he was knee deep in snow with a shovel in hand. The Mini had been left out of the shed to make things easier that morning but Adam now cursed his decision as the engine shuddered from the cold and refused to start. A path was dug so it could navigate the driveway and after Adam fiddled with things in the bonnet and his bulky cousin gave it a push, the car groaned to life, steaming as it warmed up.

'That was close,' Adam said, stamping his boots on the doorstep.

Robbie was already in the kitchen pouring them each a small measure of whiskey.

'Dutch courage,' he said, passing them to the men.

'Cheers,' Adam said, lifting his glass. 'This will calm the nerves.'

'To love,' Robbie said, raising his glass.

With Adam and his cousin gone, Robbie was left sitting in a three-piece suit in his mother's kitchen. He could hear his sisters giggling and running between the rooms above him but it was forty-five minutes later when they appeared in the hallway in matching gold satin dresses with their hair soft and their skin tanned.

'You look beautiful.'

'Wait till you see Mum,' Elizabeth said, rubbing something shiny on her lips.

'Give me your honest opinion,' Wendy said. 'Do I look like mutton dressed as lamb?'

She was smoothing the sides of the dress self-consciously and her eyes were wide and terrified. He took her hand.

'Wendy, you look absolutely gorgeous. The dress is perfect on you.'

'Robbie! My mascara's going to run everywhere,' Elizabeth said, starting to sniff.

The three of them stood quietly and a car sounded its horn outside.

'That's us,' Wendy said, lifting one of the bouquets of cream roses sitting on the table.

Robbie saw them to the door, warning them not to slip on the icy driveway. When he turned round again, his mother was standing at the bottom of the stairs. Her shoulders were squared and confident, her waist pinched by the cut of the taupe-coloured dress, which fell to the floor with netting flicking out around her ankles. Something fur sat comfortably around her shoulders and her grey hair was swept up and pinned with a gold clasp. He had never seen his mother wear anything quite so elegant. At Wendy's wedding, her skin had been pale, her eyes lifeless and her skirt suit painfully old-fashioned. Robbie remembered Elizabeth trying to convince her to wear lipstick and it turned into an argument that saw the lipstick being snapped in two and Elizabeth fleeing in tears.

'My goodness' was all he could say to his mother. She smiled as if expecting such a reaction.

'Will I do?' she said, turning full circle and giving him a cheeky smile.

'I'd say you'll do, Mum.'

'Here,' she said, thrusting a camera into his hand. 'Take a photo of me.'

Robbie looked at the pink, digital camera she had passed him. 'Is there no photographer?'

'No, no, I didn't bother with all that,' she said, striking a pose.

Robbie insisted that they get some shots in the doorway to her house. There was a wooden archway covering the doorstep, up which his mother had coaxed two yellow, climbing rose plants. The snow had formed a hood on the awning and she looked quite beautiful against the heavy wooden door.

'Come on, get in,' he said, opening the door of the Mini. 'I've had it running since the girls left to give us a bit of heat for the journey.'

He helped his mother fold her skirts into the footwell before passing her the flowers. The restoration of the car had been kept a secret until the previous day. Adam had barely said hello to Robbie's family before he whisked them on to the decking.

'Wait here,' he had said, skipping off to the bottom of the garden. Margaret had rolled her eyes but when the roar of an engine sounded from the shed, her hand flew to her mouth.

'No,' she said from between her fingers.

Adam had polished it until the red was as bright as a chilli pepper and he could see his face in the silver rims on the wheels. He drove slowly up the garden with the window down and his elbow resting on its sill. Robbie wrapped his arm around his wife's waist as his mother walked shakily to the car and started touching it. Later, over a bowl of vegetable broth, she told them the history of her very first car.

'It was the only thing I took with me from the farm, the only thing that was truly mine. It was just about driving back then but it packed up not long after and I didn't have the money, or the inclination, to fix it. In the summer of 1975 my mother died. I'd been married a year and we were reaping our first harvest at the farm. I was orphaned at the age of twenty-three and it sent me into a bit of a spin. I didn't feel ready to be a grown up but there I was – a wife, a farmer and soon to be a mother.'

She bit her lower lip.

'We weren't so vocal about our feelings back then and it certainly wasn't encouraged to worry your husband with your struggles, but John knew I was sad and no amount of fresh peas and strawberries seemed to be cheering me up. One day I was out the back hanging the washing out and I heard someone hooting at the farm gate. I ignored it at first, thinking it very rude that the person wouldn't just drive into the driveway like everyone else. Well the hooting continued until I threw down my basket and opened the gate.

'And there he was, your father, sitting on the bonnet of that little Mini Flame looking pleased as punch. It wasn't my birthday and we were months from Christmas, so I never thought it would be for me. I just slapped him on the arm and said he was a wild man for buying himself such a toy. "It's for you", he told me, and he had to take me by the shoulders before I'd really believe him. He opened the driver's door and told me to take it for a spin. He had some excuse about some farmwork he had to attend to, so I drove off along the country lanes on my own and stopped at a little clearing somewhere along the Tullyard Road. I opened the glove compartment and found a letter that said I didn't need to be unhappy any more because a girl with a bright red car surely knows her place in the world.'

After a short pause, she laid her hand on top of Adam's.

'Just seeing it all bright and red like it was back then, well, it's just incredible.'

ဢ

'Before we go in there,' Margaret said as they pulled up outside the church. 'I just want to say how happy I am that you and your family are here.'

'Me too.'

'And that I'm proud of you.' She looked down at her dress. 'But more important is that I'm sorry.' She fanned whatever he was going to say with her hand. 'We'll not get into it all now. I'm just relieved to see that your father and I didn't ruin your lives completely.'

With flowers in hand, she stepped out of the car before Robbie had a chance to open the door for her.

ဢ

When the wedding ceremony was over, guests loitered in the pews to congratulate the bride and groom. Robbie ducked quietly out of the church and made his way to the graveyard at the back of the property. Wendy had phoned him a month before to say that the headstone had been erected and he wanted to see it for himself. As he passed the older graves, snow started falling soundlessly around him, adding to the several inches already blanketing the ground. It was difficult to navigate the churchyard through the snow and his feet had turned to ice in his thin leather shoes but he uncovered his father's grave in the corner where Robbie's grandfather and grandmother were buried.

10 August 1940 – 15 June 2010
In Loving Memory of John Hanright

He scuffed the ground and looked about him. A robin landed on a nearby railing and cocked its head in Robbie's

223

direction. Its breast was bright and its inquisition welcome as the blizzard closed in and cut him off from his surroundings. The snow dulled the sound of people leaving the church and Robbie was isolated at the foot of his father's grave.

In the months between the funeral and the wedding, Robbie had not experienced the sense of loss that he had expected would come. On his return to Dublin, the frenetic pace of life picked him up and carried him along until his deadlines were met in work and the things he had put on hold had been attended to.

Although he spoke to his mother and sisters often, there was little mention of his father and it was not until he was confronted by a slice of marble with John's lifespan etched on its front that it seemed final. Elizabeth had transported the bedding plants from the farm to the grave but they were buried beneath the snow and would quite possibly not make it through the winter. Robbie removed the rose from his lapel, placed it at the foot of the gravestone and brushed the snow from the lettering of his father's name.